MISS THE MARK SERIES:

Tormented Dreams

Book 1

An Apocalyptic (End-Times) Thriller Novel

Adrienna Dionna Turner

Miss the Mark Series

Book 1: Tormented Dreams
Book 2: Outcry, Shalom!
Book 3: Souls Lost 2 the Mark
Book 4: In the Nick of Time
Book 5: Diabolical Invasion
Book 6: Bloodshed in Armageddon
Book 7: Christ Coming
Author's Site: http://www.adriennaturner.net

Guardian Watch Series: (TBA)

The Guardian

This book is a work of fiction.

All Scripture quotations and explanations are derived from New International Version; Life Application Study Bible, NKJV; The New Strong's Concise Concordance & Vine's Concise Dictionary of the Bible; and The Nelson Study Bible, NKJV.

Some passages derived from these books: Smolen, Rick. *One Digital Day: How the Microchip is Changing our World*; Malone, Michael S. *These are the Good Old Days;* Turner, Adrienna D. *Unleashing the Spirits, Vol. 1-3* (2011); and Parenti, Christian. *The Soft Cage: Surveillance in America from Slave Passes to the War on Terror.* New York: Basic Books, 2003.

Printed in U.S.A.

eBook ISBN: 978-1-945822-01-8
Print ISBN 13: 978-1-945822-00-1
Print ISBN 10: 1-945822-00-7
Library Congress Control Number: 2016912720

Dream Your Reality Prophecies (DYRP)

http://www.dreamyourreality.webs.com
http://www.dream4more.org
(Dream4More w/Adrienna Turner).

Cover design by AA Thompson II
Editor Karen Overturf

Preface

There was a record of those who never saw the fulfillment of God's promises and still never wavered.

The word *sin* means "error" or "failure." The term *sin* also means to go astray or to miss the mark. Webster defines *miss the mark* as: "departure from a known rule or duty prescribed by God, any voluntary transgression of the divine law, or violation of a divine command;"

"voluntary...neglect of duty..." The simple solution is to repent.

The goal of *Miss the Mark Series* is to stir up our awareness of the end of times during the seven-year Tribulation when the Antichrist will reign. *Miss the Mark Series* exposes those who will be judged according to God's Word; the Great Tribulation until Jesus returns; and the second coming of Jesus Christ from an urban perspective.

Prologue

Death Merges

"Sin came into the world through one person, and death came through sin. So death spread to everyone, because everyone sinned" (Romans 5:12, GW).

LES BLANCHE

Washington, D.C.,
Task Force Special Operations Headquarters

Chief commanding officer, Les Blanche's presence alarmed the Task Force Special Operations officers and soldiers to halt and salute their leader. He stood near the sound booth and stared at the HD screens in front of him. He pressed one of the buttons to playback a report of a CNN broadcast of Salvator Lothar. Les surveyed the room and studied the facial expressions and slight gestures of the men and women as they watched the shortened video on the devastating events of world destruction. Les sought after an immense outcome. He carefully observed a few officers. He saw one praying to her *God* by clutching tightly on her cross, mouth moving to a whisper unheard to her peers. Another with his eyes closed and head shifted upward as if he was praying in silence. A slight nod by another officer; Les sensed an unseen presence was in the room. He focused on Lothar's discussion but kept heed of these few officers whom he felt would be a problem. They were not proceeding with the new regulations and updated mandatory combat drills.

"You've just seen a series of videos of war among third world countries like Syria and Iraq," said Les. "Some heads of state are doing this to their own countries as a result of evils introduced by previous rulers. They enforce their dictatorship in their countries with such catastrophic events. It is time for us to reinvent our scare tactics to show these countries that we're ready for whatever they may have in warfare. Our country is known as the land of the free, and we are free to make our own decisions as a leader of weaponry."

Some of the commanding officers nodded in agreement. Others stared intently at Les. All were alert, awaiting instruction at a moment's notice.

"Therefore, as you see this man, Salvator Lothar, is our next standing world leader. He has propositioned tactics for this special force to govern a safer country and a peaceful one. We have positioned each man and woman in this room to be the first to not only protect our country but to receive the implant—this delicate but powerful device—in your bodies. Here watch this clip..." He pressed the next button. He saw their approval nods as the general atmosphere changed, but there still were a few skeptics in the room. He dug deeper into his spiritual sensor and detected that some had Christian beliefs against this proposal of the biometric chip.

Les knew he had to set the example. He needed these men to not only respect him but fear him. The next chief officer and president of the United States would unite all the nations, and also would be willing to exterminate any that didn't follow his will. After the viewing, he glorified their role, "So, you see how you'll do a great deed for our country, and set an example for others." He looked around, noting still a few who appeared to be resolute, and continued, "We will become a safer nation. We won't have crime or theft because the security measures will track every move someone who will harm us makes. This device, as you can barely see, is only the size of a mustard seed." Staring at the woman who fingered her cross, he said abruptly, "We will not tolerate any moles, traders, or those who will not take the will of our Messiah." He heard an obnoxious sigh from someone in the room. His turned his head, and his eyes went to slits after targeting the perpetrator.

On an impulse, he considered the few soldiers he eyed earlier. He sensed their rebellious demeanors while listening to the demands with frequent twitches, holding on to their hanging cross necklace, or praying gesture. He knew they wouldn't follow the new order. This new mission assigned to him by Salvator Lothar could not fail. Taking matters into his hands, he yanked the gun from his holster on the side of his belt and shot each target quickly in the head. Blood sprinkled on those who stood nearby and on the video equipment near the control booth. Not a stem of remorse coursed through his body. Screams echoed in the room as the gun blasts rang in the ears of the remaining soldiers.

One of the soldiers stepped up to him and tried to stop him, asking, "Who is the Messiah? And why are you killing good men and women? Most of us are willing to do all we can for our country, including taking this device into our bodies..."

Les shot him in the face to stop him. Blood gushed all over the man's army attire as he fell to the ground in agony, his breath gurgling through the blood pouring from his mouth.

"Now does anyone else have any comments?" Les fumed.

No response.

"Take him to the medical quarters. Get him out of here! I hope the rest of you make the wise decision, and this process will move steadily and painlessly. This proposal is the first that will take place and will become an imminent recommendation for this country to get on the good foot with our Messiah to come. Next, we will work to get ready to reinforce the biometric chip first in America using other tactics, and then many other nations will follow."

The remaining officers listened quietly and attentively, with masked apprehension, lest they too become the next gunshot victim.

"We will split some of you in various sectors for varied assignments needed in the operation, and others will be in drills to acquire new war tactics. We selected each and every one of you, specifically, for the task at hand. Make us proud. You also will be paid handsomely, as you walk that way, and follow Dr. Whitbacker. Then you will receive a white form that will disclose your salaries and revised job descriptions under Special Ops governmental higher-ups," Les said in a commanding voice and pointed in Dr. Whitbacker's direction. Dr. Whitbacker stood upright with his hands on his sides as they buzzed him in, waving the others to follow him through the silver, secured doors.

Les was pleased the first order of affairs was finally happening, and he was easily wiping out those who would refuse. He contacted a clean-up team to remove these dead bodies and prepare falsified documentation to be logged in their secured database. After they finished, he would send out officers to report their deaths to their families.

Chapter 1
Dust to Dust

ISAIAH E WILLIAMS

Florida
Saved Disciples Association

Isaiah was about to deliver a sermon on *Street Disciples and Surveillance* to warn his flock about what was occurring in their world now. His heart began thumping before he began to speak. Around the congregation, his gaze caught their calm faces, hands nestled on their laps, and some ready to take notes as he presented the lesson. He heard a couple of coughs and sighs before stepping up to the pulpit to deliver the message God had given him for these "last days" with a final warning. His lips tightened then loosened, and he licked his lips. His heart sank to think about the outcome of his delivery. Only God knew. The microphone picked up the sound of his breath as he began to speak to the hungry and eager spectators.

"We have *street disciples*, which in the older days were called *evangelists*. *Evangelists* are people who mailed material to people in the neighborhood, shared the gospel with others on the streets by going door to door. They shared the Good News with those who are in prison, on missionary trips, and wherever they go."

He closed his eyes for a moment to collect his thoughts. He opened the Bible, turning the pages. He glanced at his congregation members. He smiled inside to see some curious expressions, hungry for the message. "Let's read Matthew 28:19 and 20."

"Say that again," Someone shouted.

"Matthew 28:19 through 20." He saw the person nod. "It reads, 'Go therefore and make disciples of all the nations baptizing them in the name of the Father and of the Son and of the Holy Spirit, teaching them to observe all things that I have commanded you; and lo, I am with you always, even to the end of age.'" He closed the Bible and glanced at his notes on his tablet.

"Today, we have another tool by using our virtual reality gadgets; where The Word can be viewed worldwide in the comfort of one's home on the Internet, Satellite TV or digital cable networks. We can hand these gadgets to our participants to see a video screening while sitting in a meeting too." He pointed in the direction of the holographic image of the equipment as a few heads turned to see.

He heard a few ooh's and ah's before continuing. "We can also wire in the media through satellite beams, which transmit our material thousands of miles away. Some are viewing our sermon, right now, as it is broadcasted. However, the government has had a close watch on the media in order to control our minds and lifestyles in this one-world-system." He then pointed in the direction of their cameras streaming the broadcast for all virtual viewers, and reverently gestured to his temples on the sides of his head.

He breezed through the material, "God stated in His Word, how intelligence will surface over the world and how this surveillance intelligence that our government has to protect us is really being used to keep a close watch on all citizens as if they are *gods*. There is no longer *privacy*."

"Tell us...pastor!" Someone blurted loudly.

"What happened to our freedom and rights? Gradually, these rights are being prohibited and are disappearing as we speak today. I am talking about a tiny square silicon chip, the size of a fingernail, weighing less than a postage stamp and constructed of crystal, fire, water, and metal. Our society views this as a miracle." He coughed. He sipped on his bottle water before continuing. His throat became raw.

"Really pastor, they can do that!" One of the members said, angrily.

He continued, with the message gripping at his heart. "We tend to forget God's miracles and focus on these technological miracles. There are tens of thousands of microprocessors built on a daily basis. More sophisticated manufacturing plants claim to keep our environment cleaner and more peaceful on the Earth. Ideally, this modern microprocessor contains up to twenty billion transistors. The government's main focus with these microprocessors and transistors is the Manhattan Project and the other major headquarters in Washington D.C. where our Task Force is to build an atomic bomb. However, there are other countries that have possession of the type of nuclear energy to create a nuclear bomb if it gets into the wrong hands, like with the Iranian President." Isaiah didn't hear a peep as he briefly gazed over his notes. He flicked his finger upward on the tablet screen while scanning the material to make sure he covered everything to recruit more missionaries.

"This is why our organization has workers with the Task Force, as well as other computer engineers and technically astute members. They make sure that those who would usher in the last days are not tapped in our network or about to shut down our live feeds. We need to broadcast our message worldwide and open the eyes and ears of the many before it's too late. Other evangelists may ignore the fact that we are being watched on surveillance cameras everywhere," Isaiah commented coolly.

The seconds were ticking away. He saw some people looking confused but curious. His stomach sank with nervousness. He nodded his head after noticing several people watching every move and then continued to inform them of the statistics, "In the world of the microprocessor, the number of transistors packed onto all the microchips produced in the world is equivalent to the number of raindrops that fell in California during this last quarter. The new *Information Age* has eclipsed the Industrial Revolution and has irrevocably changed the world. This little chip has made improvements, exceeding productivity by eighty percent, and turned the world as we once knew upside down. But, it's not that far-fetched and can take another century for humankind to realize all of the new technological implications are taking place. This new microprocessor, these little silicon chips, embeds intelligence beyond man's wildest dreams despite infinitesimal demands for space and power."

"Come on." A woman shooed.

He clearly understood from the faces he saw and the loud sighs that he was losing some of the congregation with all the technological info. He heightened his tone, "This power I'm speaking about is meant to help redesign humankind, our lives, and in doing so, to enhance, *supposedly*, our human traits and our own individuality. What kind of *power* is this?" he asked, placing his fingers in the air to put quotes around the word "power."

He continued, "God granted us with free will, where we are free to make choices. He didn't want us to be robotic figures over the earth. This new technology will have total control and power by seeing and hearing everything we do. There are some of us that have already been fooled to implant this silicon or microchip in our hands, eyes, and brains believing it is the New Digital Age to go paperless and living without credit cards."

He saw a few nods. He hoped they were in agreement, then cracked his knuckles and stretched forward. One of his congregational leaders motioned him to continue. "Go ahead Pastor. Teach!"

Someone yelled without warning, "They can't handle the truth!"

"Today, there's no place on earth or in another galaxy that has gotten so far as to turn a little sliver of crystal into the digital age generation evolution. This clever technical novelty will take our very souls. *Geniuses*, one may think or say, but *are* they?" He pounded on the podium and leaned to one side to hold his weight. He noticed the pounding noise woke some from their deadly trance.

He reached for his hankie in his breast pocket and tapped on the sweat beading on his forehead. He continued his train of thought in hopes of not losing them to boredom, "Some can refer to the Global Positioning System or GPS, which you can find in aviation, our vehicles, and other custom-mapping software devices. We have scanners that speak in monotone computerized voices on our garages, in our homes, talking remotes or televisions, and so forth. Since early developments, they have setup hand scanning devices in our superstores, in our school systems, and on our laptops. They have other computer gadgets to pull up our social security number, name, other information we would normally keep on file or in our personal computers, and those hand-scanning devices locate our bank accounts and other financial institutions we're associated with in order to pay for our purchases at the cash registers. In our eyes, we've achieved great things with these devices, but in God's eyes, we're setting ourselves up for destruction." He looked out at his congregation and saw some of them had crossed their arms. Isaiah didn't want his egalitarian members to be blinded by the deceptions and devices of the enemy.

"Enough of that." He paused to make a quick glance at his members. He slightly changed the pace and tone of his voice for the recording to an upbeat momentum, "I can go on and on about things that will come to pass according to God's Word, but I want to focus today on our *Street Disciples*. How can you serve the Lord?"

"Tell us, Pastor!"

"God wants us to pray, praise, glorify, and turn to Him in everything we do on a daily basis. We need to meditate on His law—precepts—and take in—contemplate—God's ways. According to Roget's Thesaurus for the word, *contemplate* means 'consider, purpose, reflect upon, study, think of, think about seriously, and plan.' To sum this up, we need to consider God's Word, to take it in our daily lives. God will show us His purpose in which we should reflect upon by studying and being familiar with God's Word. We need to think about God's plan for our lives by taking it seriously. If we obey, imagine how much we'll be blessed and satisfied."

He heard a few *Amens*. He noticed a few stern looks. Some folded their arms and others crossed their legs. "In 1 John 1:8, we should be able to admit that we have sin. Deceive ourselves and the truth is not in us. If we confess our sins, God is faithful and just to forgive us of our sins and cleanse us from all unrighteousness.

Allow God to reveal your faults, shortcomings, mistakes, and sins to you," he paused.

The hardened stares encouraged Isaiah to continue to explain what *sin* truly is and hoped the Word pierced their soul like his had been during these perilous times. *"Sin* is one's desires, fulfilling the wants of the flesh, and willingness to proceed with an act, thought, or desire for oneself. We're doing things according to the world, of the flesh, and not seeking the Holy Spirit for guidance and direction. Before making decisions and doing things, seek God first, to direct our path, decisions, and everything that we do in the name of Jesus Christ and His will. I should be doing according to God's will in my life and willing to hear clear instructions from the Lord. I should also decipher right and wrong in everything I do, especially things that are not like You, Lord," he boomed, raising his arms and eyes toward the large cross hanging from the ceiling.

"Let's turn to 1 John 3:22-24, and bookmark your Bibles to Luke 11: 28 and John 14:21." He cautiously glanced at his congregation as he assigned people to read these scripture passages.

Afterward, he prayed to end the service. Surprisingly, no one conversed with him about the lesson when he left the platform, and he pondered on what it meant. *Did they get my point?*

He stepped to the church doors. He stood at the threshold. Some scampered past other members to leave the building without even shaking his hands or greeting one another after service while others gave him the obligatory, "Good sermon, Reverend." Isaiah then overheard in passing, "I'm supposed to believe that hogwash on invading my privacy!" The other person shushed the negative commentator. He couldn't place the face.

He gave it to God that they got the full message and hoped they left with a good foundation. He stepped outdoors and gazed at the dark clouds. He felt the presence of God. His expression softened, and a faraway look took over as he contemplated the future. He could smell the immediate storm in the air, and considering the future turned his smile into a grim expression. The coming storm between God and the world saddened his heart. He knew darkness was soon to fall. The enemy already had scales on the people's eyes; they would see what their hearts desired, and not the will of God.

Could his Street Disciples, in this atmosphere, proselytize new converts to Christ?

Chapter 2
Awakened by a Nightmare

ROYA WHITMORE

Florida
Whitmore Mansion

In the dream, Roya visualized hurricane storms outside of her home. The misty winds were thrusting and howling one hundred-forty-five miles per hour with blinding rain in the dusk night. Cold sweat dripped from her forehead. Tears trickled from her eyelashes. The gusty winds were nearly blowing the abode away. There was an immense cloud with flashing lights. In the center of the cloud appeared a fiery image that looked like a glowing metal. Suddenly she was standing inside, and outside her windowpane, the winds had such a powerful force that the trees swayed back and forth, while other homes on the block were drifting in mid-air. Some of the homes blew into the ocean nearby. There were also cars swirling in mid-air, as the fearful winds of the storm were moving closer and closer to her home sweet home. She was amazed at how calmly she looked upon the storm and found herself praying, "Lord, where can I hide or run? Oh Lord, could this be Hurricane Katrina?"

She then noticed a male image in the midst of the grayish clouds. She blinked several times, thinking the figure would vanish and only turn out to be a figment of her imagination. At the same time, she could see a mile or two away from her vicinity. Homes and buildings were in shambles, only leaving debris and darkness behind. The man's ominous gray, cat-like eyes bored into her dark-brown eyes, reading her thoughts. She felt a tapping at her soul, taunting her emotions. *No voodoo crap!* She screamed inside.

The male image drifted closer and closer to her. Noticing his smooth cream complexion, wavy jet-black hair, and keen features, her eyes blinked shut, but she could still see the male figure in the gloomy sky. Hauntingly enough, his mouth uttered words followed with a devilish chuckle. The diabolical figure kept repeating, "Follow me. Follow me. I'm the true Savior. I can protect you...safety is at hand...peace on the rise."

A short pause, then his snake-like voice changed, soothingly saying, "Let me in your heart, mind, and soul. I'm the truth and the only way! I will prove who I am to you soon."

His voice escalated to nearly a yell, "But when you wake up, you will catch your adulterous husband in the act! Ha-Ha-Ha-Hee-Hee-Ho." He ended with a creepy chuckle.

Whoa, what a Roya! Could this be real? Girl, wake up! This dream felt so real. *Could this be a stratagem or diversion?* She extended her hands to the male image floating in the murky night sky. Shouts of her twin boys came from the man's mouth.

Her eyes popped open. Her heart was beating crazily, and she was gasping for breath. She put her hand on her chest in an attempt to settle her thoughts. *Dang, was this a spiritual revelation or a warning? This dream could have a connection to a futuristic reality. Will this stuff happen in the near future? Perhaps it's a dream coming from God, telling me something I needed to know!*

She clearly heard Tavon and Javon's verbal rage from the living room over a *Speed Racer* game on a hyper-virtual-dimension visual

✝ 15

card. Her sons had fought before over a computer game displayed on the sixty-inch plasma screen with hypermedia.

Her daughter, Joy, shook her shoulder and whined feverishly, "Mom, get up."

A baby was moving and swimming in Roya's womb. She was in the third trimester of her pregnancy. She tried to ignore her children's screams, and hoped her husband would amend their behavior. She stretched her arms, and a yawn roared from her lips. She still smelled the potpourri candle that was lit from last night. *Solomon has to be roaming around the house and not paying attention to our children!* Blowing hot air from her mouth, she thought, *dang, why hasn't he made sure those kids ate something?* The clock read 12:01 p.m.

"Solomon, Solomon. Solomon! Where are you! Do you hear me?" Roya fired and blinked.

Joy sat on the bed, stared at her mother and repeated, "I'm hungry." Her stomach hummed.

"I heard you. What's wrong? You're nine. I taught you how to cook. Where's your father?" Roya asked.

"I don't know, Mom," Joy moaned as she waited for her mother to spring out of bed.

"What do you mean, you don't know? I guess I'll have to get up. That husband of mine! He could've reached for a new box of Cheerios, at the very least. Anyways, it's getting late, and I need to fix something to eat. Why couldn't you or the boys cook something to eat earlier?"

"Umm no, they ate most of food in the fridge, you know what you always say," Joy pouted and pursed her lips as she shook her head with her hands on her hips, *"growing boys."*

Roya sat upright in bed and leaned against the bed's headboard. She hugged Joy and slid down the side of the bed. Her slippers were at the edge of the bed, and she slid them on. Joy kissed her mother on the cheek and then on her lips. She smiled, hoping her daughter didn't smell her morning breath. She mustered up the strength to walk out the bedroom door and saw the lights on in the master bathroom. She stepped in the bathroom. Joy followed her mother, leaned, as if weakly, on the wall, lowered her head and stared at the floor. Roya looked down at her and saw the sad expression on her face.

"Sweetie, I heard you. I will fix you something to eat. Since I just got up, let me use the bathroom and wash my face and brush my teeth if you don't mind?"

"Mom!" She blurted loudly with her lip puckered.

"What!" Roya threw her hands up in the air and couldn't believe her daughter raised her voice.

"I'm sorry, Mommy. Okay." Joy lowered her head, pouting out her bottom lip after she saw her mother's eyes bulge, nose flare, and hands on her hips with head tilted.

"I was just asking myself if you were speaking sassy to your one and only mother that gave birth to you and was in labor for nearly eleven hours!" She pointed her finger, wiggling it. "But, I know that God has a plan for your life, Joy. You will be Mommy's singer. Don't think I don't hear you singing along with those gospel songs I play on the radio. Also, I'm gonna sign you up in the choir ministry offered at your school." Roya flushed the toilet and washed her hands.

"No. Okay, Mommy. I'm sorry. I loo-ve you," Joy said, answering all of her mother's questions at once.

"Okay, I love you too." Roya kissed Joy on the cheek after brushing her teeth.

Roya knew in her heart and mind that she was raising her children to love and fear the Lord. Additionally, she wanted to bring her children up with manners and discipline in a godly way. Tavon and Javon stopped yelling once they heard their mother's toilet flush and the sink water running. The twins pretended they were getting along and well-behaved when she walked into the living room.

She tilted her head and glared at them. "You two need to stop! I know y'all were arguing over that game again. I will remove that game out of the house if there's a problem again!"

"No Mom, please don't!" They said in unison. "We won't—" Roya knew their line of defensive word tactics.

"I don't want you to occupy all your time with game anyways. We'll read a Bible story later today after I'm done cooking something to eat. Or we can watch it on HDTV. Did you two eat yet?" Roya asked, nicely.

"Nooooo," both answered in unison.

"What? I don't know what's going on with your father! Plus, you boys are old enough to cook something to eat. Why are you waiting on me to do it? Ugh. You could've made your sister a bowl of cereal at least. It's noon!" Roya barked, and marched past the living room to the kitchen after scolding her sons.

Her sons shrugged, with the I-don't-know-look. They were so focused on the video games and not what time it was. Roya dug the frozen food out of the freezer and popped it in the microwave. She handed Joy some dishes and told her to set the table for lunch. Then, as the microwave bell sounded, she sent Joy to check on her brothers while she started frying the defrosted hamburgers and potato wedges in the hot grease on the stove, and then opening a can of corn.

"Children, come and eat!" Roya called, once she finished cooking lunch.

Tavon and Javon threw down their Wi-Fi controls and stormed into the kitchen. The clamor of their feet sounded like elephants.

"What did I tell you about running in the house? We can't eat until we say grace. Who'd like to say grace?" Roya asked, hoping one of her kids would volunteer or she would have to say it.

"I will, Mom," Tavon said, as he pulled out a chair to sit down. He waited until his other siblings were seated with their heads bowed, eyes closed, and hands folded for grace. Roya smiled and nodded her head at Tavon when they were ready.

"Dear God, we want to thank you for the food we are about to receive. Thank You in Your name, Jesus, Amen," Tavon said quickly, ready to dig in the food, instead of saying a longer profound prayer.

"No, you should've said the one that we learned in school. God is good. God is great. Let's thank the Lord for the food on our plate..." Joy said.

She was cut-off by her mother as she nodded her head, "Forget it. You didn't volunteer. Let your brother say grace his way, as long as he's thanking the Lord for our food. Joy, you can say grace tonight for dinner, okay?"

"Yes, Mom, okay." She proceeded to eat her food.

The smells of the food made Roya feel a little queasy and unable to eat her cheeseburger. She tried to finish her fries and corn, but felt as if she was about to vomit. The twin sons recognized their mother wasn't feeling good. They stopped eating, got out of their chairs and began to rub her stomach. Tavon was on the right side and Javon was on the left side.

"Baby, you need to stop making Mommy sick." Roya glanced down at her stomach, speaking to the fetus growing inside her womb.

"Yeah, we love Mommy, and you too, baby," Tavon said, rubbing his mother's navel once he lifted up her flowery shirt.

"See, we're playing with you, baby, from the outside by touching Mommy's stomach. Can you feel that?" Javon words followed after his brother's, rotating all around his mother's basketball-like belly.

Roya smiled and hugged her boys close, "Yes, if it doesn't work for the baby, it sure makes me feel good. Thank you."

Joy removed herself from the dinner table to walk alongside by her mother to hug her. Once Roya sat down in the living room, Joy was only able to put her arms partly around her mother's belly. She laid her head on Roya's lap.

"I love you kids. A mommy couldn't ask for better kids. Just because I don't feel well all of a sudden doesn't mean you guys have to stop eating. Go ahead and finish your food," Roya countered and motioned them to go back in the kitchen to eat.

Roya's children obeyed her orders to sit back down in their seats to finish eating. After about ten minutes, she called to the kitchen, "one of you clean up the plates for me, okay?"

She smiled as she heard the garbage disposal start up.

She spoke in as clear a voice as she could, and the television reacted incorrectly. Again, Roya spoke with clarity, "TV turn on, flip to CBN, hold channel," to turn on the virtual-audio-functioning-digital television to see what was on Christian Broadcast Network

(CBN). *Not perfect,* she thought, grabbing the remote. Manually, she started flipping through the channels. She finally was amused by the program aired on the Gospel Network. She heard the beautiful melodies and rhythms from the gospel soultress. The soultress singer slowly paced across the stage, moving gracefully as her arms swerved in the air from side to side. Her tailored-made white gown swayed with her body movements, smiling and singing. Roya loved the gospel hit song, *Heaven.*

Suddenly, a flashback of the dream came upon her eyes. She glared into the distinctive male sleek eyes, as the image inched closer to the house and objects flew in the air like a tornado. *Who could this man be?* The doorbell rang, and the vision left her. "Joy, answer the door for me, sweetie. Mom's still sick."

Tavon ran to the door. "Who is it?" he asked.

"It's Grandma!" he yelled, and yanked open the door.

Roya smiled at her mother as she walked gracefully into the house. Javon ran to his grandmother and hugged her, jumping up and down with his brother. After kissing both boys, making sure to leave wet kisses so they'd wipe them off with their shirt sleeves, she looked for the little one.

"Where's my Joy?" asked Jewel, and Joy walked in from the kitchen.

"Here I am, Grandma," she said and giggled as her grandma spun her around.

"Regular young lady, helping your Mama. I am so proud of you."

Javon and Tavon started dragging Grandma to their rooms.

"Look, Grandma, see what Mom did in our rooms while she was getting the baby's room ready!"

✝ 21

Jewel gave the children the treats she carried and walked back to the living room.

"Roya, listen. I heard about your husband is working with a new artist. I think his name is Jay Z, no, I mean Jay-Zo, dang, what is that kid's name? I believe it's J-a-i-z-o-n. Yes, that's it," her mother spelled his name.

"No, Mom. Sorry, I was hypnotized by the spiritual sultry on TV. But I heard you. Oh, his name is pronounced Jay-zhon," Roya corrected her and "zon" sounded French, almost like "John" in English.

"Well, as I was saying, Jaizon resembles Solomon so much that women mistake him as your man. Girl, you better think twice about this mess. They're trying to accuse Solomon for cheating in the *National Inquirer*." She pulled the paper out of her Coach bag and handed to Roya. "Look at the picture. I also seen it aired on *Entertainment News* last week," Jewel said and pointed at the picture with her forefinger.

"What are you talking about?" Roya's face wrinkled. "Are you saying they're accusing my husband of cheating on me? Do you believe those stories in that *National Inquirer* anyway?" She threw her hands up in disgust. "There might be some truth in them stories, but there are more lies in that magazine than meets the eye. Anything they write isn't factual information since they write only half of the truth and spice their articles up with mostly lies for entertainment." She shooed and fanned herself. "Biblically speaking, a lie is an outright lie even if it has some truth to it. Therefore, I don't want to look or read that article! Plus, I only watch the Gospel Networks." She grunted and turned her head, so she would not see the article and photo her mother was raving about.

"Alright fine, sweetie. I just thought it was rather interesting." She closed the paper and placed it on the table. "Do you still need me to watch the kids so you can go meet your husband at the beach house studio to see what *is* really going on for yourself?" Jewel insinuated.

"Mom, you can be rather atrocious and sarcastic at the same time! You can sleep in my room or the guest room, your choice," Roya struggled to get up.

"How can you say such a thing?"

"I'm glad you're spending time with us, regardless of your accusations. I don't want you to leave."

"Roya, I know that you're having some complications with *this* child. I want to be here to make sure you're alright and deliver this child naturally if it's God's will. I don't want to lose you nor that child in your womb." She sighed heavily. "However, you and Solomon need to slow down on this baby-making-machine. The twins are thirteen years old now, and Joy is nine, now you're on child number four at your age. It was fine when you conceived the twins at close to twenty-four years old, but now you're thirty-seven," Jewel griped.

"Mom, God has total control over my health, my body, and the life I carry in my womb. You act like I am 40 or something!" She threw her hands in the air in disgust. She shooed her mother's comment with a loud sigh, "Once I met Solomon, I knew in my heart and mind there was nothing I wouldn't do for him. He did everything in his power to win my heart over and to make me fall in love with him. He easily succeeded. It was a difficult journey since I had to deal with those groupies and worried about other women stealing my man from me since he was in the spotlight as a producer

✝ 23

and actor. As time progressed, I learned to trust him; at least I thought I did until you brought this mess to me about him possibly cheating." Roya explained, reassuring herself that he couldn't be cheating.

"Where is all this coming from?" Jewel shook her head. "I'm not saying that, dear. I'm simply saying they've mistaken him due to Jaizon's resemblance to him. As your mother, I'm just warning you, and I don't want anyone to hurt you. You are my pride and joy. You're all I have left after your father died in the war," replied Jewel.

Roya wasn't sure how to respond to her mother and sat silently. She saw her mother's familiar authoritative stance and decided to barge ahead.

"Mom, I made sure our relationship was secure first before bringing children into this world. Plus, in the Bible, Sarah had her first child at the age of ninety, and Abraham was like a hundred. I'm not even half that age! Furthermore, my doctor said that I was in good condition to have children." Then her voice lowered to a whimper, "But with this pregnancy...yes, I'm a little worried. I was put on bed rest because the doctors were afraid I would have a miscarriage. I had to lie on my back in that bed for over a week and drink a little red wine to build my blood up. I thought I was going to lose this child, but our Heavenly Father tells us not to be anxious for anything. Maybe this is nothing to worry about."

Feeling drowsy, Roya stared down at her stomach for a long period of time, wondering what God had planned for her life. "I'm going to lie down, Mom." She sauntered in her bedroom and plopped on the bed. She lay on her fluffy white pillows, and scooted over to make room for her mother.

Her dream returned. The winds were powerful, fierce, and whistling as cars, homes, and trees blew everywhere. In the dark skies, Roya recognized the diabolical male again. Then, she heard his distinctive, baritone voice as his head moved toward her window. His head shook until she realized it would separate from his body like a magic show. As she glared at the face she began to think it might be the Antichrist, or Satan, and suddenly the head was bodiless. Suddenly the features became clearer, and heard his loud voice, and the head shrunk so that it could move to her ears, somehow on both sides, like earphones. Then she was listening to its voice.

She woke up suddenly, shaken up a little. She climbed out of the bed and looked outside the windowpane, praying that her dream wasn't on instant replay. Thinking about what she read in the Bible and hearing God's voice during her meditation time, she reached for her Bible. It wasn't resting in the usual place on the chest in the bedroom. She glanced at the bed. Jewel wasn't near her on the bed. Roya tiptoed in the kitchen, opened the refrigerator and the voice spoke. *"Your husband, Solomon, is cheating on you. As we speak, you'll be caught up in the storm. Not only will you drive through the winds blowing you off the road, once you arrive at your destination, you will see and hear your mate cheating. What will you do? Will you kill him? You brought cheating up while you dated him. You said wouldn't tolerate cheating. You went to drastic measures to get your point across. Now go and see it for yourself!"*

She argued with the voice, "There's no way he could cheat. He loves me. He had other opportunities to be with the woman of his dreams, but I was his dream!"

She glanced at the children playing in the backyard as she sipped the water.

There was no storm like a hurricane she saw in her last two dreams, even though she knew Florida was known for frequent storms. She felt a sudden coldness, as if someone walked right pass her. She didn't believe in ghosts. She raced back to her bedroom and turned around to see the Bible still resting on the oak wooden chest. She toddled to the shelf of books to pull out the *Book of Dreams*, to gather a logical explanation.

She still heard the voice. "Listen. As I stated before, your husband is cheating. He will call you to check up on you to see how things are going. It's late. But he will make an excuse to stay later. He will engage in some sexual activity. Hurry up and get there! Now!"

Roya giggled under her breath. 'Yeah, right.'

She woke when the phone rang. She quickly ran to the phone. For a moment, she apprehensively wondered who could be on the other end of the line. She found herself staring at the picture of the *Last Supper* on the clock dials pointing at the Roman numerals. *Whoa, did I sleep all those hours, thought I would just take a short nap and it is 1:00 a.m.* Roya picked up the digital phone with video conferencing option. She adjusted the settings to audio and video to see who was on the other end. Solomon. *Boy, is this a coincidence.*

"Hi. Why aren't you speaking? What's wrong? You look like you seen a ghost. Baby, talk to me." Solomon said.

"Umm. No. I had a crazy dream. Do you know what time it is?" *Why is he calling at this hour? He should be next to me in bed.*

"Yes. That's why I'm calling to see if you were asleep."

"Solomon, you're worried about me being asleep. Why?"

Solomon heard the change in her tone, as well as watching her face take on a defiant look. "Roya, I didn't want to wake you. But, I wanted to leave you a message letting you know that I'll be home late. I didn't anticipate being here so long," smiling from east to west, looking so innocent, but sneaky. *Boy, you are in trouble, mister. What are you hiding? Why are you acting like a one a.m. phone call is normal?*

Roya didn't respond. She blew a kiss over the phone to play off her suspicions.

After disconnecting, she double-checked on her kids to make sure they were still asleep. Then, she glanced in her room, ready to grab her jacket and shoes. She moved quietly and carefully in the hallway, down the stairs, and avoiding sudden moves so she wouldn't awaken her mother. She spotted her mother lying on the couch with the television on.

Exiting out the front door and locking it behind, Roya walked to the garage. She activated the garage door, "Door open."

She whispered to herself, 'Do not forget to close the door.' She listened to the device babbling in her car, thinking, *will this thing shut up? I don't want the neighbors or my family to wake up from this noise.* Backing her new Galaxier out of the driveway, Roya watched the automated system close the garage door after pressing the yellow button in her car. She turned on the radio, hearing an "oldies but goodies" station, and listened to the voice command GPS while driving down the road. The radio station was playing, *Secret Lovers*, a song her mother played in the early 1980s, when she was a small child. She was familiar with this old school R&B classic jam.

Moreover, she prayed that Solomon wasn't making love to a secret lover in the beach house. The beach house brought back

✝ 27

memories in her subconscious mind, a place for wining and dining while they were courting. After their marriage, they remained in the beach house until they had children. Mostly made out of wood, it looks like logs on the sand, near the ocean. *What a beautiful outdoor view, looking at the ocean.* It had a beautiful indoor landscape with a Persian rug in the living room, fireplace, lighting such as lanterns and other fixtures that are button operated instead of voice command features, and theatre television. It was only a two-bedroom home of which one of the rooms was a recording studio. *I miss this home. But, once I got pregnant, he wanted bigger and better.*

Her daydreaming vanished. She no longer focused on memory lane as she got closer to the cabin. A storm blew up while she drove. *Oh, Lord. That dream is coming to life, for real. I'm trying to steer this car since the automatic driver isn't working.* Roya felt sharp cramps in her lower abdomen. *I hope this baby isn't thinking about fighting its way out of my womb. I'm not due for at least six weeks.* Fear engulfed her so much that she forgot to push the "sea option" button on the dashboard inside the car. Hard raindrops came down from the sky at a rapid pace. She squinted her eyes while the wipers swished.

"Stop!" She screamed and prayed that she'd make it to her destination safely. "Lord. I need you more than ever. Please don't forsake me. Please let me arrive safe and sound to the beach house. I love my husband. Please Lord; don't allow me to see the worst. I pray Solomon's remaining faithful to me. Please don't allow this car to act up or caught up in this storm. Oh God. Oh God! God! Help me!"

The storm swept the car in the opposite direction, wind thrusting, and twirling. She could only think about the safety of her life and unborn child. Only one block away, suddenly, the storm stopped and she slowly drove into the driveway. Quickly turning off the music, she stepped out of the car saw the security lights turn on automatically as she crept up to the house. For some strange reason, the door was unlocked. *Why would he leave the door unlocked and cracked open?* Carefully and slowly she tiptoed through, and quietly closed the door behind her. Her breathing labored, she nearly hyperventilated as her nerves and curiosity escalated. *Breathe in, breathe out. Breathe in, breathe out.* She spoke in a low voice.

She then heard giggling from a female's lips, and heard a male's voice speaking but sounded like gibberish. All her thoughts escaped her. Her emotions stirred, anger ready to unleash. If she was a cartoon character, horns would grow from her head and flames from her nostrils and ears right now. Anger and asperity filled her soul, but she shook hastily to stay focused. She exhaled to a whisper, "Calm down, girl. Or you'll lose this child. You'll go into labor before the time."

Stepping closer to the bedroom, her awareness heightened. She noticed the studio door was slightly open. Music was playing, but the harmony of voices came from the bedroom. The song being played tugged at her heart. She tightly gripped at her shirt, touching her chest. He wouldn't dare play music to lure the woman into the bed. Her mind lingered on the couple gyrating. She glanced over her left shoulder, and inched closer to the bedroom to get a look. She felt a lump in her throat. Wait! Solomon played smooth sultry music to woo her. She swallowed hard. She felt foolish to not trust her better half—her husband. Curiosity leaped at her heart, wondering if Solomon was cheating! She thought, *men do lie and then will cover*

✞ 29

their dirt. Would he deliberately hurt me? I can't imagine being without him. I don't want to be foolish like Ashanti sings. My heart can't take no more. My body feels like it wants to crash.

The bedroom door was open. Roya's eyes widened. *There's a black slip-on by the door!* She slowly looked further into the room. *Trousers and pants on the floor, with a red silk blouse on the bed! And there's the other shoe near the bed.* She imagined the couple racing to the room, undressing and kicking their shoes off. The female pair of shoes was laid side-by-side; shiny, ruby red stilettos at the lining of the bed. *Are they in the shower, our shower, or our Jacuzzi? Champagne in the bubbles, like we did when we were first engaged?*

Roya's eyes scanned the dim room and noticed the patio screen doors were halfway open. She heard whispers followed by laughter and smacking of lips. *That trick can't be kissing the lips of Solomon, my man. She can't be kissing on my husband. Solomon is my lifeline; my provider; my babies' daddy; my head of the household; my best friend, lover, and soul mate until death does us part. I meant what I said in our vows.* Roya's thoughts felt jumbled. Stealthily she looked outside.

Is that my dress she's wearing? That dress looks just like the one I wore last year. Roya backed up and turned around to the walk-in closet to see if it was where she left it. *Yes! They've been through the walk-in closet because dresses are scattered everywhere.* Roya saw the woman's trashy clothing near her foot. *Ugh!* She kicked the outfit away from her feet. *Am I dreaming? Wake me up! Please.* She rubbed her eyes to wake up from this fantasy. Then, she smelled the scent of *Baby Phat Goddess.* Her heart started beating rapidly. *Yahweh, help me!* She started fanning herself and quickly stepped out into the hallway. She heard the door slide open and laughter as the couple came in from the patio. *Same thing we did in the past. We watched the sunrise when we were courting. How dare he? Welch's champagne instead of a bottle of Monet. When did he start drinking that?*

"I do want you. I do," she heard the woman moan.

"Oh, I see that you do. I'm ready when you are!" he replied in return.

As the romantic duo was about to interact in lovemaking, Roya couldn't stand anymore. She looked through the open door and saw a honey-brown skinned woman, and admired her shoulder-length curls with blonde-highlights. She replayed the memory of seeing her designer clothes on the floor near this woman's trashy attire. After catching *her man* in the act and in the company of another woman, Roya was about to lose her marbles and self-control. *Love is patient. Love is kind...*

Roya decided to sit on the floor. She gasped for air. *Kill them. Kill them. Kill them... What, "Psycho?" No, I'm about to go Looney Tunes, any minute.* She stood up and then ran to the kitchen to grab a butcher knife out of the kitchen drawer. Then, she stormed into the bedroom, holding the butcher knife in her right hand. The handsome, mocha-coffee complexioned man whom Roya believed was Solomon jumped off the woman. Her eyes narrowed at the sight of *supposedly* Solomon. He had grown a lightly-shaved goatee. His skin tone lightened a bit and red-toned, *it must be the lighting.* She shook at that notion. His eyes slanted but seemed more oval-shaped than normal. He appeared slightly younger. The woman purred. *He looks younger. He must have taken a spa treatment.* He then leaped over the bed on the other side of the room near the computer desk to get his clothes.

✝ 31

"Please don't kill me," he begged, "I didn't mean to do anything..." as he rushed to slip in his pants. He slowly walked backwards past Roya with his white t-shirt in his hand. She allowed him to walk out. *Did Solomon meet her at a concert or a dinner date? Now, they had a few drinks and Solomon brought her back here?*

"Trick. Where do you think you're going? You're not getting out of here alive!" Roya sneered.

"Why me? Is that your husband or man? He told me that he was see-gal." She stuttered and continued, "I meant single. I didn't mean to mess up anything. I was led astray and believed him. What can I do to make you not hurt me?" pleaded the woman, holding her hands in the air to block her face.

Roya toddled towards her slowly with the knife angled to cut deep into the flesh. She stopped and lowered the knife, and backed up.

The woman hopped off the bed and attempted to grab the sheet.

Roya went blank for a moment, allowing the naked woman to dodge past her. Roya dropped the knife and went into the walk-in closet. She retrieved a gun from a shoebox. She opened the barrel. It was loaded.

"How could I let this trick get away with murder?" Roya spoke softly in the walk-in closet, watching this woman grab *her* designer dress.

Roya walked out with the gun, aiming it at the woman as she began to put the dress on. The woman fell back, waving her hands as she saw the gun.

"I'm so sorry. Please, I didn't know that you lived here. I thought this was a place to chill with..." the woman's voice trailed off.

"Does it look like I'm in the mood to hear that crap? Tell that to someone who'll listen." Roya stepped closer as the girl looked over her shoulder at the door.

Roya silently thought, *My man is well-known in the public eye. Solomon's a hip-hop and R&B music producer, CEO of Soul Man Entertainment recording company, mogul, and icon in the music industry. Who doesn't know him? I don't know who this broad thinks she is, coming up in here and messing up a happy home. I could just wring her neck. Everything is about to tumble down. Down they'll go!* She fidgeted, and her hands shook.

His voice sounded different, maybe because he was scared and voice was at a higher pitch than usual. This honey-brown woman has the nerve to hold onto her clothes and cover her body. Roya aimed the gun to fire. The woman's weave fell off as she dashed swiftly around the corner. Roya pursued them. She pulled the trigger. One blast; and smoke from the firing of the gun. Gun smoke filled the air, and Roya choked from the fumes. *Dang, why did I close my eyes when I fired the gun?* When she opened her oval eyes, she realized that she hit had him in the leg. In slow motion, she watched her man fall to the ground. She tiptoed closer to the helpless body in the semi-darkness. *That has to be my man, Solomon. Is it?*

"How could you shoot me? I know that we were wrong to make out in your place, but I only stayed around until Solomon was done working on my track. I knew that he'd be in the studio a few more hours to master the track. I figured since he'd make a few calls and work on some other tracks, and I'd make myself at home. He always told me that I could eat or drink whatever I wanted!" His voice elevated to a high-pitched cry.

"What did you say? Who are you? You're telling me that you're not my husband, Solomon? Darn." She slapped her thigh. "My mom tried to tell me that he does resemble you, but I didn't want to hear...or believe her. Oh, my. What am I going to do? So you're that guy, Jaizon?" Roya shrieked.

"Yes, I'm Jaizon. So, you're his, umm, wife?" He squeaked in his pain.

"Yes. I thought you were Solomon! I'm terribly sorry! Please forgive me," Roya fell to her knees. Roya put the gun down at her side.

Now, Roya's lips quivered. *He does resemble Solomon. But his eyes were dreamier; he was sexier and slightly different complexion she refused to accept earlier.* She sensed that the woman would call the cops. *Then, I'll go to jail. I can't go to jail. I'll be locked away for life for pre-meditated murder. I really lost my self-control. My emotions are on a limb. I was about to kill both of these people. Poof, I knew that I couldn't deal with the fact if my husband was cheating. I can't make this go away, no abracadabra. If I go to jail, I'll no longer be with my husband or my kids. I don't want to leave my kids. I don't want to have my babies behind the prison walls. Then, my child will be removed from my arms into some other families' lives. No.*

"This couldn't be happening to me. Lord, please help me. I'm so sorry. I should've listened to you or, at least, waited on you to speak to me," Roya softly spoke, as someone reached behind her, to take the gun from her side. She turned around to see who was standing behind her.

Solomon picked her up and held her tightly against his racing heartbeat.

"Roya." He stole a glance at her, then Jaizon's bloody wound. His face was strained. "What have you done!" His face flashed fear. "What have you done?" Sunlight beamed through the window blinds. It was morning already. Roya saw Jaizon lying on the floor, as the blood drained from his leg. The heat intensified throughout her body, and she began to sweat. Everything was spinning. She knew her blood pressure was too high.

Jaizon whined, "Please call someone. Ambulance, hospital, help me, I'm bleeding here to death. Solomon, I can't believe your wife shot me! You told me so many good things about her and how you wanted me to meet her. This is how I meet her, shooting at me!"

Solomon went quickly to the kitchen for a first aid kit. He disinfected and bandaged the wound.

"Hush, it's just superficial. I'm sorry for my wife's behavior, but what are you still doing here in the first place? Who is she? She attempted to run out my front door, but was unable to disarm my security system that I put on about twenty minutes ago," Solomon pondered with his hands rested on his waist and waiting for an answer from his recording artist, Jaizon.

Jaizon's woman spun around to answer the question, "Oh, I'm Pammie. Pamela. I wanted to kick it with him. He called me on my cell phone to meet him here. I thought this was his spot." She smacked her lips like popping gum, not eyeing Roya, and struck a punch in Jaizon's arm. Her eyes glanced at Solomon, and her voice rose an octave, "I didn't know it was your place! I didn't know she

✝ 35

was your wife! So, if I understand this correctly, she thought Jaizon was you. Wait, you are Solomon!" She fanned herself with excitement. "Hold on. Soul Man Entertainment that has signed multi-platinum rap artists and you've been in movies like...umm...uh, I can't remember the name of that flick from back in the day," she stuttered. "My roommates won't believe that I met you. Maybe this is an awkward time to ask for your autograph! But, your wife is totally loco." She pointed at Roya and then made a circular motion near her temple to emphasize the word *loco*.

"I can't take back what I've done. I'm truly blessed that I didn't kill anyone. I'm so sorry for the misunderstanding. Oh Lord, I heard a voice telling me that you were cheating," Roya replied frantically.

"What? You mean *woman's intuition*? I hope you're not talking about hearing voices in a psychotic way?" asked Pammie, as she twisted *her* designer scarf around her fingers.

"Wait," Roya retorted. "You didn't help the matter any. Why would you wear my clothes?"

"You have beautiful dresses from top designers that you see on TV and seen in videos, so I wanted to feel like a superstar. I didn't mean any harm. I'm willing to take them to the dry-cleaners if you like. I don't want to get shot over that." Pammie explained, placing one of her hands on her hip and waving the other with attitude.

"What? What did you say? You'd take my clothes to the dry cleaners and never get them back!" Roya snapped back, inching closer.

"Calm down ladies. This is getting out of order. Jaizon, I can take you to the hospital on my way home, if you wish." He shot a glance at his wife. "And, Roya, you're coming with me! We can talk about this later." He turned to Pamela. "Pamela, Pammie, or

✝ 36

whatever your name is, my wife has apologized. Apparently, there's a misunderstanding; that's all." He then turned to Roya,

"Roya, I can't believe that you'd pull out this gun. You never held a gun in your life! I'd never cheat on you. Now I know how you'll respond if I even thought about it," Solomon exclaimed.

"No, you didn't say that to me. That if you cheat on me, this is how I'll act. Am I hearing you correctly, Solomon? I made a mistake. I always told you that I couldn't imagine you cheating on me and no telling what I'd do. Please forgive me for thinking the worse. Plus, my mother told me that this guy resembled you and I didn't want to hear the rumors she repeated earlier. I also didn't believe that you were cheating on me, until..." Roya tried to explain.

Solomon interjected, "Then, why did you do this?"

He bent forward to help Jaizon off the floor and Pammie helped on the other side to lift him up. Jaizon limped as he walked, and Roya followed. She didn't want to answer Solomon's questions. Instead, she hinted with her facial expressions for this woman to take off her stylish attire and put on the trashy outfit still on the floor of the bedroom. Solomon understood her, and nodded his head. *Don't worry about that dress.* She knew the designer dress Pamela had on her slender body cost over a thousand dollars.

After helping Jaizon in the Cadillac Escalade, Pammie's gestures indicated that she was anxious to leave. She watched as Pammie backed up her car and drove down the road. The storm had stopped. *No more gusty winds blowing or hard rain. Pammie is gone.* Thinking back, Roya realized she had been contemplating pulling that trigger and killing them both. God had heard her plea for help. 'Thank God,' Roya mumbled. *Solomon stood behind me to retrieve the gun.* Now, she was watching her husband driving to the

✝ 37

nearest hospital with Jaizon on the passenger side. Roya desperately wanted to say something, however, it wouldn't change the fact she shot Jaizon.

He glanced over his shoulder to speak to Roya, "Baby, you thought that was me! I was in the studio finishing up a couple of his tracks. I didn't think Jaizon would bring a woman to my house to make out." He glared at Jaizon, "Jaizon, did you call her from one of those hotlines? Where did you meet her since we were together most of the day? Well, you know what I mean. Was she a call girl or one of those escorts?"

Jaizon gave a blank stare.

"Man, what were you thinking? How could you do that! You got my wife thinking you were me. Wait a minute, what were you doing here at this hour, in the first place?" Solomon questioned and pounded on the steering wheel.

"Man. She isn't a call girl or escort. She's my recent girlfriend. Pammie is a nurse-in-training. She's still in school. I wanted to see her since I know I'll be on tour soon. I didn't mean to start all this mess in your place! Sorry, man. I didn't know that your wife would come up in the place going berserk," Jaizon explained.

"What? Oh well, if you had the kind of day I had, you'd be acting crazy up in here too!" Roya fired back at Jaizon's comment, "Do you know you're making rumors of Solomon cheating, and the tabloids have pictures of you all over? The very least you could do is tell them directly who you are! No wonder they think you're Solomon if you're going around using his place for a rendezvous," she fumed. She couldn't wait until she was able to go home. The rage bottled inside exploded as she pleaded for sympathy, "I had a dream telling me you were cheating on me! When you called, and you weren't home, I wanted to see it with my own eyes to make sure I wasn't imagining. My mind was playing tricks on me." She threw her hands over her head. She turned to her husband. "Solomon, I really thought Jaizon was you. My mother was right, he does resemble you, and her talk probably fueled that dream."

They exited the car, and Solomon helped Jaizon to a wheelchair near the hospital entrance. Once they were inside, Jaizon hopped from the wheelchair and limped to the reception desk to see about his leg. He shook his head at Roya in disbelief. Roya fell to her knees crying and asking for forgiveness.

"I would never cheat on you. I take my vows seriously. I love you dearly. You don't trust me?" Solomon said softly. He held his hands tightly on the wheelchair steel bars.

The nurse at the reception desk earshot overheard their conversation and smiled, saying, "Aw, that's so sweet."

Solomon glared into the nurse's baby blue eyes as she combed her fingers through her long, stringy blonde hair and pushed it behind her right ear. Roya saw the two looking at each other for a brief moment, and whacked a slap across his arm to get his attention.

"I don't trust myself. I thought I was seeing *you* cheating on me. All this time, it wasn't you. I could've killed them. I would've ended up pulling the trigger on myself, losing my happy home because I thought he was you!" Roya cried. Her face was flushed. She swayed to the side, and Solomon held her to stand upright. He walked her to a seat. She fanned herself.

After Jaizon had filled out the paperwork, he shook his head 'no' when the nurse asked, "Do you have any medical insurance?"

Solomon responded, "I will cover any costs that he has for this doctor's visit." He glanced over his shoulder. He then turned to the admitting nurse. "I may have to check on my wife too."

The nurse gave a nod. "She looks flushed. I see she's also far long in her pregnancy. We can run the normal tests." She offered kindly.

Solomon signed the forms indicating he would cover any costs for a doctor visit, X-rays, and any other fees that applied. The doctor reentered in the waiting room to reassure Solomon and Roya.

"I'm Dr. Vangstalling," he said, shaking their hands, "The bullet skinned across his leg. We were unable to find a bullet anywhere. We also did X-rays to make sure there was no piece of the bullet. He'll be in a lot of pain, so I've given him a pain killer, and I'll prescribe codeine to relieve some of the pain. Otherwise, he's free to go. He can have a check-up to make sure it's healed okay. He has a few stitches. If you have any questions, feel free to call the hospital." They stared at his reddish-tone complexion and noticeably bi-focal glasses, as he wiped his hands on his white jacket.

Solomon turned to the nurse in the room, "Let me know when Jaizon comes out so I can take him home." The admitting clerk motioned them to follow her to an empty room. "The nurse will be with you shortly."

"Thank you," Solomon said.

"I'm fine." Roya insisted.

"You do not look fine. I'm concerned about you." He looked at her stomach. "And the baby."

She agreed with a nod. The nurse stepped in and checked her pulse, ran other tests, and informed her that her blood pressure was slightly high. "Thankfully you didn't have a panic attack based on

✝ 40

the readings. Did you notice any sharp pains in your chest? Hard to breathe?"

Roya shook her head. "No, to both of your questions."

"Your doctor may want to do a check-up since its 140 over 90. Normal levels are 120 over 80. If something is stressing you out, I advise to rest. Take deep breaths and try to relax."

Roya glanced at her phone vibrating. She received a text from her eldest son.

"Thank you, doctor," Solomon exclaimed. He turned his gaze from the nurse to his wife. "What is it dear?"

"Just a text from, Tavon, wondering where I'm at." She answered and lowered her head to finish reading the text. She replied after swiping the letters on her smartphone. '@ hospital. Be home soon. I'm fine.' It buzzed. 'Ok. Call me when u leave. Luv T.'

"I suggest making an appointment with your doctor to avoid having your baby early."

"Okay," Roya said softly, with a reassuring nod. She knew she was highly upset at Jaizon, and it still lingered. She rubbed her stomach.

The door closed. Solomon rose to assist Roya. Both slowly walked to the waiting room.

Then he asked the nurse where the bathroom was, as she pointed him in the direction. "I'll be right back, Roya. I need to wash my hands after Dr. Vangstalling's rubbed his hands on his lab coat. Ugh." He cautiously wiped his hands on his jacket as a natural instinct. Roya slightly nodded her head and dug in her purse for hand sanitizer to disinfect hers. She sat in the waiting room, tapping her feet against the tile. She softly said, "Lord, please help me get through this. If Jaizon decides to press charges, this could get ugly. I hope he sees that Solomon is trying to make it go away, which I thank you for."

Jaizon's leg had thick white medical bandages to cover his small gun wound, and he hopped while taking baby steps with his crutches. Solomon stumbled a bit when he came out of the bathroom. He bobbed his head when he looked at Roya. He spotted a wheelchair, and wheeled Jaizon out of the hospital and assisted him into the Cadillac Escalade as Roya placed the crutches in the backseat. Solomon strolled in the hospital with the wheelchair and left it in the front entrance as he ran back to the car.

No words were exchanged during the drive to Jaizon's house. During the drive to the beach house, Solomon asked Roya, "Are you able to drive home okay?"

"Yes. I'm fine now. I've calmed down. I'll meet you at home."

"Okay."

"I love you, Solomon."

Roya entered her car after observing Solomon drive off in the sunrise. She stared into the sky, admiring the sunrise, hues of yellow-purple-reddish colors. She took deep breaths.

"Dear Lord, I feel like I can't come to You after what I've done. I was wrong, Lord. I should've trusted You. You asked me to read Your Word, but I only stared at that Bible in my room. I was afraid to pick it up, not knowing what I could read in Your Word to help me. I know Your Word is *Basic Instructions Before Leaving Earth*, but Lord, I'm glad that no one died this morning. Lord, please forgive me. I pray that my husband won't be upset with me and will be able to forgive me. I trust in You, Lord, that You'll make everything all right. Thank you, Lord, for listening to my prayer, in Jesus' name I pray, Amen."

Chapter 3
More than Meets the Eye

SOLOMON WHITMORE

Florida
Whitmore Mansion

Solomon parked the car in the garage, and the garage door descended. The doorbell blared. He raced through the home from the garage door entrance to the front door and opened it without thought. He then flagged the kids to go upstairs. Jewel followed and shook her head to indicate she'd look after them.

Once Roya arrived home, she saw police cars were parked in front of her home with their red and blue lights blinking. She parked her car next to Solomon's in the garage.

"Hi, honey. We have company." Solomon forced a smile when Roya came in.

"I see. I saw the police cars parked in front of the house when I pulled up." She said dryly.

"Ma'am, we'd like to ask some questions." The officer said.

Roya motioned for them to have a seat while he held tightly on his ballpoint pen and pad of paper. He sat and finished his informal discussion, "Your husband answered our questions, but the complaint was against you. We have a witness who states you tried to kill her and her boyfriend, Jaizon Wright. Is this true?" asked the short husky police officer. The other officer stood at the ready, surveying their home.

Roya sat. She stuttered and stumbled on her words. "I didn't kill anyone. My husband was there. Didn't he tell you everything already?" Roya replied, rubbing her sweaty hands and placed them on her lap.

Solomon gave the officer a brief description of what happened there. He paced back and forth as the two police officers stood in one spot to scribble the information on his small notepad and the other officer observed both Solomon and Roya for any unusual facial expressions. Roya agreed to go down to the station for further questions.

She was handcuffed and taken to the police station. Solomon pleaded to go with her, but he was completely ignored as they left.

"Solomon, why did they wheel my daughter to the police station? What did she do? She had handcuffs on." Jewel inquired as she stormed down the stairs.

"Mom, I'm searching for my lawyer's phone number to get her out of this mess. It was a *mad* drama. I don't have time to explain since they're interrogating her as we speak." He attempted to dodge his mother-in-law to contact his lawyer.

"What do you mean? You better give me some answers this second," Jewel fired back.

"Jewel. I really want to get down to the police station with my lawyer present for this ordeal. Also, can you watch after the children when they get out of school before I return?" He begged.

"Sure. But honestly, the boys are old enough to take care of themselves and watch their younger sister. You guys *baby* those boys! I'll gladly watch my grandchildren, though. But will you answer my question first?" She sassed.

"Okay. Jewel, Roya had a crazy dream that caused her to come to the beach house in Fort Lauderdale. I had no idea Roya was even there until I heard the gun fire and Roya screaming. I had one of my artists, Jaizon, in the studio earlier recording a couple tracks. I was laying out the tracks...uh...mastering his songs." He waved his hands. "Jaizon called some woman to come enjoy his leisure time without me knowing when he was supposed to leave. He claims she was his girl; I think her name was Pammie. Roya found them in the room together got the gun from the closet, and shot at them." He explained rapidly.

Jewel flagged at him to slow down.

He collected his thoughts and said calmly, "I'm blessed that she shot his leg and didn't kill the man. Man, come to think about it; what if that was me. I wouldn't be standing now." He lightly touched his chest and looked downward. "However, Pammie left last night in shock and phoned the police. I think she's pressing charges."

He continued fiercely, "I'm not sure if she can do so since she was a stranger in our home in the first place. Also, Roya said that Pammie was wearing her expensive gown, and she refused to take it off. She drove off with the dress still on while we took Jaizon to the emergency room. Despite the fact, I'm also glad that I came in time since Roya might have pulled the trigger on her next! She was awfully snippy." He gasped loudly.

"Are you serious Solomon? All this happened..." Jewel gasped and covered her mouth with her right hand.

"I don't know what I'd do without your daughter. She's my life, my better half." He dazed into a trance for a brief moment. "Now, can I contact our lawyer for this matter?" Solomon gave an off-the-wall look at his mother-in-law, waiting for her approval. Jewel emphatically nodded her head.

She yelled out the front door as he backed the car out of the garage, "Go and help my baby!"

He speedily drove to his office. He shuffled through papers before going to the police station. He kept dialing his lawyer's number, waiting for Mr. Bronson to pick up. Finally, Solomon made arrangements to meet him at the precinct.

Chapter 4
Dead Memories

JEWEL BATTLE

Florida
Whitmore Mansion

As Jewel prepared lunch for the children, she thought, again, about the story of Jesus raising Lazarus from the dead. She wished she knew what happened to her husband, Lazarus. There was no logical explanation why Lazarus Battle was deployed to Iraq and later stationed at military headquarters in Iran. *Power? Control over the oil?* The media left Americans high and dry with snippets of the Iraqi war with American troops fighting an ambiguous war. Nuclear energy: some toxics in Iran. *I'm still confused over it all. I miss his arms, his presence. He always told me he deserved a "Jewel" when I told him he was my "Rock" from God.*

Will I ever find someone like him again? The dating scene isn't the same anymore from speed dating, video conferencing, online dating services, hotlines, instead of old-fashion dating like courting. Come on. This is not Stella got her groove back. I know that God will bless me in his own time. And I know that I'll see Lazarus again when I reach Heaven!

✝ 47

She then called the kids to eat. Lowering their heads for a moment to pray over the food, they picked up their forks in silence, and ate.

Jewel sat upright and rubbed her chin, thinking that she had to be right about her suspicions. Lazarus' death was a setup; more than just a war and hoped to unleash the real mysteries behind it so his soul would rest in peace. She would also have peace. She dazed into a daydream with her eyes wide open.

Chapter 5
Charges Dropped

ROYA WHITMORE

Florida
Police Station

At the police station, Roya was processed, and the interrogation process began again. The burly officer reviewed the file report. He told Roya that Pamela pressed charges, not Jaizon. *Maybe I can say self-defense? What can I do? What is Solomon doing? Oh Lord, please help me.*

"What is this all about? Do you think this is special treatment for a celebrity, by coming to my home personally, to arrest me? Then, you arrest me over someone who was in my home without permission. What about breaking and entering into *my home?*"

"Our report tells us that she was welcomed into the home by her boyfriend, Jaizon, and you started shooting like a madwoman and shot him in the leg and about to shoot her next. She was unable to escape the premises because of a security alarm. Is this true, Mrs. Whitmore?" the officer read the report to her, and his eyes narrowed at her for a response.

She gathered her thoughts and chose her words carefully before answering. "Whatever she says isn't true. First of all, she shouldn't be in my home unannounced. You can verify with my husband that he was unaware of her being there. Jaizon was a guest that took matters in his own hands to invite that woman to *my* home."

"Ma'am...you say *your* home. But our records show that the property is under Solomon Whitmore." He said abruptly and shuffled the paperwork in front of him, and then eyes glared sternly at her.

"What are you implying?" She paused as her eyes widened. "Solomon Whitmore is my husband. What's his is mine! We're married!" Her voice rose sassily. "Anyways, there should be a law against intruders and unwelcome guests." Roya insisted. "I was not expecting to see what I saw. She had my thousand-dollar dress on. Did she tell you that?"

She waited while the police officer completed his report. She heard her husband at the front desk of the police station requesting and demanding to see his wife.

"For the last time, where *is* my wife, Roya Whitmore? We have our lawyer present and would like to see her now!" He roared. He stood, waiting for a response from the front desk representative at the police station.

Roya stepped out of the office and stood against the wall near the door. She saw that Solomon's lawyer was apprising Solomon to allow him to handle this situation. Mr. Bronson, Solomon's attorney, spoke. "Officer, what are the charges against Roya Whitmore, Mr. Solomon Whitmore's wife?"

The officer replied, "Mr. Bronson, upon questioning Mr. Jaizon, we have determined that Mrs. Whitmore is not guilty of the accusation made by Pamela Amanda Righteous. She is free to go."

Roya walked toward the officer at the desk when she heard him tell Mr. Bronson the news.

"What about my dress? Have you arrested her for stealing my dress?" Roya inquired.

"Ma'am, the dress is being delivered to your home by the cleaner," the officer replied.

"She knows my address? How will it be delivered to my home?"

"When we took the complaint, Ma'am, we asked the woman if she was there by permission, and all we could get from her was that her boyfriend invited her. We did have to detain you until we had determined the truth. You and your husband both said no one had permission to be in your home, and that your husband armed the security system. The officers then took possession of the dress and delivered it to the cleaners. She does not know where you actually live." He passed a pad of paper to jot down her address.

"Was she going to mail it to the beach house?"

He didn't respond.

"So is that all you need from me to get my dress?" She asked, tilted her head.

He nodded and put the pad on the desk to contact the cleaners.

Solomon hugged Roya tightly to where she felt she couldn't gasp the oxygen in the air. She reached up to plant a kiss on his cheek and said, "Baby, calm down. I'm glad that you made it down to the station. No charges were pressed. I see that you brought your lawyer on the scene."

"I wasn't going to take any chances. Who knows what these cops will do to you? For some reason the law keeps changing and enforcement is no longer here to protect and serve, they seem to be under some regulations to serve the president and not the public. There are some new procedures, and I was afraid they'd find a reason to lock you up behind bars. There are discussions on the news and media that martial law may be enforced soon and there are some very strict rules that impact our faith. For example, I think a law was passed to inject a chip in people at hospitals for medical reasons; for judicial reasons to keep track of our movements, actions, and our offenses and charges or warrants for arrest. Crazy stuff like that now; and now they're discussing a plan to insert that in our children at their schools. We need some kind of privacy! It might not have been long until you were injected with that chip," remarked Solomon, as some of the officers in the station overheard his allegations.

His attorney, Mr. Bronson, pulled Solomon by the arm, requesting him to leave the police station abruptly.

Roya observed them and tried to eavesdrop as Mr. Bronson explained his rush in a private section outside of police station, looking over his shoulders and up to see if any cameras were around. "Mr. Whitmore, you are right in only part of that. HIPPA, The Health Insurance Privacy and Portability Act, was replaced with a Verichip implantation in the guise of creating a *private* record of someone's medical status since there have been so many high profile releases of information."

Solomon gave him a blank stare.

Mr. Bronson continued without glancing at Solomon. "These biometric IDs can be placed in one's finger, eye, or hand with a voice recognition system and are able to view a person's identity through the iris by retina scanning, and able to see through the eyes every person and experience one encounters. Once you take this implant in your body, every thought spurred up in your mind, and every action you take the World Order documents."

"I got it, man," Solomon said.

Mr. Bronson stared into Solomon's brown eyes, "The laws and regulations on this Verichip device are still being finalized."

"Yes. I am fully aware, Bronson. Why are we discussing this here and now?" Solomon raised his hands.

"I want you to understand your actions clearly. Citizens who believed in privacy and their rights under the Declaration of Independence, which Congress passed on July 4, 1776, are fighting against the implantation as another form of slavery. These American people believe in dissolving the political bands and assume the powers of the Earth are between Laws of Nature and God, not man. Moreover, as I do, they believe all men are created equal with certain unalienable rights—life, liberty and the pursuit of happiness."

Solomon interjected, "I see. So this gives the American people the right to abolish this *new government* if it's not laid on these principles. We've lost ourselves and need to return to the original plan of our forefathers." He clicked his finger like something clicked in his head.

"Look, there could be allegations taken against you, my client, for making such remarks against the judicial system like you did back there in the police station. You got that?" He pointed his forefinger in his face, between his eyes.

Solomon lowered his head, trying to ignore Mr. Bronson's knowledge of historical and constitutional factors in the briefing. Mr. Bronson's voice rose, "This could be major since they were undergoing a few new laws and Congress passed new regulations and procedures that shouldn't be discussed in public!"

"Fine, man. I got it! I think you are taking this political reasoning over your head, man. So are these new regulations finalized?" Solomon hissed with a twinge of anger in his voice.

"As we speak right now, these regulations are becoming laws since Congress signed on the dotted line," he said jokingly.

Solomon's facial expression didn't soften or chuckle.

"First, it started with our Voting Rights with the Supreme Court ruling, and now this." Mr. Bronson rambled and walked to the street, headed for the parking garage. Roya noticed he was sweating profusely, and he wiped his brow with the back of his arm. She shook her head. *Luckily, he's not wearing white!*

Solomon folded his arms and stood upright. Roya read his non-verbal gestures, seeing that his anger was still brewing, and his nose flared with eyes twitching. Roya then noticed passers-by and tugged on her husband's shirt to get going.

Tormented Dreams

Chapter 6
Groundbreaking Changes

SOLOMON WHITMORE

Florida
Saved Disciples Association

Solomon had already known about the Verichip since he secretly had joined a group called Alliance Crusaders for Christ. He had kept this undercover and a secret from Roya. *Why did I go off like that in the police station? I knew better!* The leader of the organization was Isaiah Williams, who also ran independent channel broadcasting about the microchip and 9/11 attacks.

Solomon knew that Mr. Bronson trailed back to his office to handle legal affairs because his phone beeped and noticed he'd received the invoice of the billable hours via email as PDF on his Smartphone. He also received Bronson's voice message concerning the ordeal that happened earlier at the police station, which was tracked and monitored at the Task Force Affairs Headquarters located in Washington, D.C. He knew the TFA was secretly established to monitor citizens' movements and illegal or unethical actions under the government's nose. He silenced his phone by turning it off before Roya asked questions during the ride home.

Solomon wanted to stop at the beach house to get a clearer understanding of what happened earlier. He didn't want his mother-in-law to hear their conversation, and more importantly, their children. Some things, they agreed, shouldn't be discussed or overheard by their children. He truly believed in being a leader and head of the household. He also was preparing them for their safety when apocalyptic events will take place and knew it was nearer than anyone expected.

Roya looked at him. *He has such dreamy, sexy, brown eyes.* He knew she wouldn't focus on a word he said as her lips formulated into an O. He tilted her head upward for a kiss.

"Roya, were you listening to me?" he tilted his head in a questioning manner.

"Huh?" Roya said, clueless.

"You didn't hear a word I said?" Solomon questioned her.

"Umm. Yes, of course, I heard you. I'm sitting right here looking at your face," Roya said sarcastically.

"Then, what did I just say?" Solomon asked, waiting for Roya's response. She followed with a giggle.

"Oh, you're trying to play me for a fool, huh? I've been with you for what fourteen years now."

"What are you talking about Sol?" She exhaled deeply.

"To some degree, I feel I know you by now. You think that giggling will take me on another tangent and forget what I asked you. Not. You need to pay attention and explain to me what happened earlier," Solomon slapped his palm

✝ 57

against the cherry wood desk in his office in the beach house.

"Solomon, I thought it was clear what happened. I thought that artist, Jaizon was you, and you were cheating on me." She was obviously repeating herself from earlier. "I thought my world was upside down, and I was losing the man of my dreams. The man I want to spend the rest of my days and life with. Do I have to go on?" She paused briefly, to catch her breath.

Solomon shook his head.

"I didn't want to lose you in the arms of another woman. I told you how I felt about sacrifices I would have to make once we got married, but I wouldn't tolerate that fact that you'd cheat on me. Especially if I'm being faithful, I'd expect the same in return."

"I didn't and wouldn't *cheat* on you." He threw his hands up.

"I completely lost it. Okay." She gasped. "I was going to shoot you and then myself."

"What would make you think of such a thing?" He shrieked.

"But I thought about our children. I couldn't imagine someone else raising our children. For example, our children being placed in the foster care system or under this new order system in some detention, or concentration center. Then, I couldn't imagine losing the child in my womb."

He exhaled, "Thank God!"

"The whole nine, shall I continue? Why do I love you so much?" Roya expounded on what took place earlier.

She rambled on about when they got married in D.C. on a whim instead of waiting to do an extravagant wedding in Los Angeles. "I'll never forget how you couldn't wait another day to marry me while I was in D.C. signing contracts for a movie deal with Warner Bros. The movie was based on *Mystic Fantasies Open Wide,* my best-selling and award-winning novel." She bragged and eyes lit up.

"Where are you going with all of this?" Solomon asked.

She smiled widely, "Now that I think of it, you even had the marriage license from Los Angeles faxed over to be signed and returned by express mail. But the private, small wedding ceremony took place at the Justice of Peace, downtown; in the central hall with my Entertainment attorney, Nichole Washburne, and your executive manager, um, whatever his name is as our two witnesses." She chuckled at the thought.

Solomon smiled cheerfully as his eyes glistened. *Her life has changed from tragedy to happiness, and to be in love with the man of her dreams.* He knew that—she told him numerous times. God sure does work in mysterious ways.

"I love you, more than words can express. I wouldn't do such a thing. All I ask is for you to trust me, besides to love me, Roya. I'm here for you more than you'll ever know," replied Solomon, as he reached for her and pulled her next to his lips, kissing her passionately.

Solomon finally kissed her and engaged in that lustful desire. He undressed her with his eyes and caressed her close to his smooth chest. The rest of the day was spent intertwined in lovemaking, and his plans to address any questions were forgotten.

Chapter 7
Scared to Death

ROYA WHITMORE

Florida
Whitmore Mansion

"That's why I'm here; to make sure my baby is okay. You're my only child, and I'm not going to allow anything to happen to you," Jewel stated with confidence.

"Don't worry. I won't allow anything to happen to me since it's all in God's will. I love you as much as you love me."

Jewel flashed a smile.

"As far as the *National Inquirer* and other gossip magazines, they will do almost anything to get a story. I don't have much faith in any of those magazines since they're simply trying to ruin my wealthy African-American husband's reputation. Who, by the way, is one of the top music producers, artists, and actors in the industry." She sounded laudable as she continued to speak commendably with her chin upward and chest puffed, "I vowed to love him till death do us part. My Solomon knows my vows: I will love, honor and cherish him, and all that crap, but don't let me catch him cheating on me! I'm going to snap and leave without any questions!"

"Really, Roya." Jewel shook her head.

Her tone changed, and then topic ventured on a biblical concept. "The Mosaic Law speaks strongly on infidelity or committing adultery which is the reason to divorce."

"What's your point?" Jewel questioned.

"I want to be with him forever until God takes us in His Heavenly Kingdom."

Jewel nodded in agreement.

"On the other hand, I hope we'll be in the Rapture with our beautiful children, and of course, you too, Mom! Or still together as a couple before the Tribulation. That's my dream," she paused as a tear rolled down her cheek.

Jewel's eyes were watery. Roya could sense her mother was wondering why she was speaking about the *rapture* and *tribulation.* Her heart thumped, "Mom, I never asked you before, but why did you name me Roya?"

She waited for Jewel's answer as she watched her eyes. She shared Jewel's passions about marriage and adultery, but she believed God was in the equation of her life, marriage, and future.

Jewel heard Roya's concern in her voice because she tightened her lips then softened them with a pucker. "Funny that you'd ask such a question, I knew this day would come. I thought I couldn't conceive or have children after being married to your father. It was five years of marriage and still not pregnant with child. I thought I was barren like Sarah, then I continued to pray, and a miracle happened. I had a dream and saw you. Later, the doctors let me know that I had an embryo living in my womb. Once you were born, I decided to follow that revelatory dream and named you 'Roya,' because dreams do come true. I later discovered your name means 'dream, or vision' which you clearly have done in this time and day, revealing dreams and visions from God, like Joseph who could look into the future through his dreams."

Her tone heightened and changed subject unexpectedly, "Then your father had to fight in a war that made no sense to me. The former president had American troops, including my husband, fighting in a war for what; to demonstrate his power like Achilles? But it was the Iraqi war that killed your father, shipping him to the States in a body bag. They wouldn't even let us see his body at the funeral, casket closed."

"Wait, Mom. What are you talking about?" Roya unhurriedly stood from her seat to reach for her mother.

"That is why I prayed for a world leader like the one we have today. He came into office too late, after the fact that your father died in this unnecessary war. What did we fight this war for; oil? Now we're in the age of energy efficient tactics. Some will ask, 'will we really see change?' Yes, we can!" Jewel rambled on, ignoring her daughter's gestures and alarmed glare.

Then Jewel came back to her main focus, "Back to your father, Lazarus wrote a letter talking about the birth of his Roya—you, baby. He loved you dearly, and you have a remarkable resemblance to Lazarus. You could be his twin.

Then, I see that you named your daughter after you...Joy, your middle name. She is a joy to be around and such a joy to the world like you are, my gifted one," Jewel added, teary-eyed with excitement.

Roya knew how much her father loved his baby girl and only child.

"Yeah, I guess you're right, Mom. Let me tell these kids to go to their room instead of sleeping on the floor and couch, and I'll rinse these dishes off and straighten up the house a little before Solomon comes home," Roya said. She tugged on Joy's arm to wake her up to get off the floor. "Come on, Javon and Tavon! Time to climb in bed!"

Jewel pushed Roya back and refused to watch her daughter try to pull Joy off the floor being seven and a half months pregnant. Joy stood up, rubbing her eyes, and swung her arm around Jewel's waist. Jewel woke up the twin boys in the living room and made them walk to their rooms. Roya shook her head after seeing her sons slouch and slump toward their rooms after Jewel pointed in that direction.

Roya then waddled into the kitchen to finish washing the dishes. After washing the dishes, she noticed that her mother hadn't returned to the kitchen to finish conversing after putting the kids in their beds. Minutes later, she found her mother resting in her bed. Roya gazed at her mother's beauty. Jewel had a creamy butter-pecan complexion, almond-shaped eyes with a slight slant, a long pointed nose that fit her face with perfection, small curved lips, and a beautiful smile that sparkled. Her hair was jet black, cut short to maintain an unruly curly-wavy texture. Roya remembered her grandfather had similar features and hair.

She sauntered back into the living room and glanced in the mirror hanging on the wall, and she had to agree with her mother. There wasn't much of a resemblance to her mother. *I look like my Daddy.* She started to go down memory lane, reluctantly thinking about her parents' nationalities. Lazarus was blessed with Blackfoot Native and African blood flowing through his veins. He had slanted eyes that could pass for being Chinese, keen cheekbones, medium-large lips, pug nose, and thick arched eyebrows. He had been muscular, athletic, and stood six feet tall.

Roya only stood five-foot-three inches, taking after her ancestors; her maternal grandmother standing at only four-feet-eleven inches. Jewel was a blend of Irish, English, African, Spaniard, and Cherokee. Roya reminisced, remembering when she ran into her father's arms as a child, and also when her mother cried all afternoon because the military officer had come to the door with the dreadful news of Lazarus' death. *He never had the chance to meet his first grandbabies, Tavon and Javon.* She shook her head and sat down on the couch.

Roya scanned through the channels. She paused on one of her favorite channels and held the remote. "There are over one hundred and eleven million Americans who carry new mobile hypermedia phones. They are tracking devices to locate the user," she heard. She laid the remote on the couch and settled in to listen.

"There are networks of transmission points which monitor and rate the phone's location whenever it's turned on. These records are stored. Some of these phone companies that were subpoenaed claimed that it was 'data mining' only for commercial uses. We're living in an Information Age of Terror, and HIPPA isn't relevant to our new privacy act. Our government states it is used for emergency purposes and for tracking mobiles in real-time by building GPS, known as Global Positioning Systems. These chips transmit the gadget's geographic location to 24-Pentagon monitored satellites to track users as they move. There are ubiquitous, 'routine,' digital surveillance records. They are created by the usage of our credit cards, bank cards, Internet accounts, memberships with the gym, and library cards. It has replaced our health insurance records, work place ID badges, or anything else that has a magnetic stripe or a code of numbers." His eyes stared as if he was reading a teleprompter.

"Electronic files can log our movements, schedules, habits, and even our political beliefs!" The speaker's voice rose. "Next, they're moving to biometric system to avoid the usage of paper money, credit cards, or any type of those cards that I mentioned earlier to a chip that'll be implanted in our bodies. This will be about money." His fingers rubbed together as he spoke about money. "They claim this new chip for HIPPA is to safeguard your privacy. It is not. They will use it to control the money. This demand will require you to sign the paperwork after the birth of your child, read the fine print, since they will implant this device inside of your newborn child, without you even realizing it." A clip flashed on the screen of the implant placed in a newborn.

"Throughout financial difficulties and economy collapses, we are to trust God entirely, especially since our

✝ 65

economy is changing the way money is distributed through electronic mediums. Soon, we'll be unable to buy or sell without this chip inserted in our right hand or head. How will we manage? Will we sell out? Call me now with your responses," the speaker said as the direct phone number flashed across the screen.

Roya swore to herself that she'd seen this male speaker before as she scanned through channels. She continued to listen.

"Many of you are wondering where this emphasis is on monitoring and tracking each citizen. After the terror attacks on September 11, 2001, in Washington, our leaders sought answers to strengthen our security and surveillance. They wanted to stop such terror attacks in the future. Instead, our troops were sent to fight Iraq for oil. You should read about the great devastation inflicted on Iraqi people by the Crusader-Zionist alliance. Americans have repeated the horrific massacres by sending our troops over to their territory."

Images flashed on the screen as he spoke, "We're fighting terrorism, as our former President stated ages ago, and Saddam Hussein issued a statement on the U.S. led Afghan war. There was an aftermath of the Pentagon's operation called 'Desert Fox' in December 1998 when Bin Laden called on Muslims worldwide to 'confront, fight and kill' Americans and Britons. We, Americans, supported leaders to make decisions to attack Iraq. There was not a formal indication or link between Laden and Saddam Hussein! But, our country blamed Iraq for the attack in New York when our Twin Towers went down. Who has the muscle or the power?" He paused with the question blinking on the screen.

"There are other countries such as Iran with nuclear power and weapons that can wipe us out in a heartbeat! Yes, Osama Bin Laden has been killed, but the enemy is still on attack!" He pumped his fist in the air. "We cannot believe there isn't any more evil lurking in the midst. Listen, Americans, there's an 'Office of Special Plans' or OSP, some sources call them 'Special Ops' or 'Special Operations' which is a secret operation aside from the Task Force military operations. One of their missions in secret relies on defectors. Check with your local news or cable network to see the time and date to watch it. You don't want to miss it. Closing, Isaiah Williams, pre-paid televised Christian Network programming. Contact information is listed below. Thanks for your comments and calls today. Good night."

Suddenly, as the quietness arose, except for the sound of the television on low volume, a distinctive male voice blurted out. It sounded more like a whisper. Roya thought she heard a voice speaking out loud. The raspy voice of a male, calling her name three times: *Roya. Roya. Roya.* No longer a whisper, it now grew louder. Not a yell or shout, but it was definitely louder. *Was it in my mind?* Roya could feel her heart racing and beating rapidly. She stuck her finger in her ears to make sure she wasn't hearing things.

Stupidly, she responded back. "Yes, are you calling me?"

"Yes, my child, you can hear me, Roya. Don't be afraid, for you're hearing the voice of the Lord Jesus. I told you fifteen years ago that you would bear twin sons. This has come to pass. Your twin boys should be raised in the eyes of the Lord. I want them to be spiritually challenged and remain in the Holy Word. Why are you afraid of reading My Word?"

Silence.

"I know the answer, but I want you to open your eyes and realize what you are doing. Your sons will grow up to be wise men like Samuel and Peter, but will become the two wise prophets mentioned in the Bible—another Moses and Elijah. You have been afraid to study My Word."

She lowered her head and nodded slightly.

"You go to church periodically, only to hear the Word, but do you put it into practice in your daily life? You say you love Me, but do you follow My commandments? You will be tested. Then, you will open what you fear the most, My Word. Put your sons in a Christian school, which I will direct you. Let them be filled in the Word, and they'll grow up to preach and teach and reach others!"

"Are you saying they're going to be *pastors*, Lord?" Roya asked. She could still hear a low voice speaking to her spirit.

"More than pastors, they will be My prophets, burning with fire from their mouths. You can refer to the *two witnesses* in the book of Revelation."

"Whoa. Since You're speaking to me, Lord, will my mother be blessed again with a husband? She doesn't want to admit that she's lonely after losing my father in the war. What...who am I carrying in my womb this time?" Roya said anxiously and waited for a reply from the Lord.

"Yes, Jewel's on a path of preparation. She'll face many trials and tribulations beyond her grasp. Jewel will only have to seek Me, and the desires of her heart will be fulfilled. Don't worry, my child, about the concerns of your mother. You'll have five children. You'll be blessed with two of a different kind. Don't be anxious for anything and don't rush this pregnancy. But, they'll come sooner than you will expect."

"What do you mean, God?" Roya questioned. There was no response. "Are you there, Lord?" she said aloud.

Instead, Jewel responded in her sleep, "Huh?"

Roya lowered her voice to a whisper and said, "Nothing, Mom." She knew God is omnipresent, but she was unable to hear His voice this time. Boy, what a dream and now this. What a revelation from God Himself! Roya looked down at her belly, knowing she carried a second set of twins in her womb. God has plans for her mother too. God has a plan for her twin sons to be the wise prophets who will preach to God's people. *Thank You, Lord,* she prayed. *I am ready, and I will see where this journey ends.*

Chapter 8
Caught up in the Midst of Things

ROYA WHITMORE

Florida
Whitmore Mansion

Roya awakened from a similar nightmare the week before. When she screamed, it alarmed Solomon. He held her close to his chest, whispering, "Sweetie, it's just a dream."

She hugged Solomon as he turned over.

Her eyes wandered instead of drifting back to sleep. She felt the cold snares from an olive-complexioned man with dark features beaming down on her. She jumped out of bed to find answers by surfing the Net, and came up short. She skimmed through the gift she received at Christmas a couple of years ago, *10,000 Dreams Interpreted: An Illustration Guide to Unlocking the Secrets of your Dream Life* because she needed answers. She turned the night lamp on. She sat down at the desk, placing the book on top, and looked in the table of contents, then the index. She read the term *hurricane* and her eyes scanned the words: *close to trouble*, and was distracted by the turn in *an affair. I spied on a sexual affair, trouble landed me nearly in jail, and I could have lost my husband, my family, and my unborn children for that crime. Lord, have mercy on this soul.*

Then a voice spoke to her spirit, letting her know that the man she was seeing in the dark shadowy clouds was Satan. Roya looked up these terms: *Devil* and *Satan* which dreams foretell that there will be *'dangerous adventures'* and *'forced to use a strategy to withhold honorable appearances.'* She read on. *The Devil as a large, imposing dressed person is a fair warning that unscrupulous persons are seeking your ruin by the most ingenious flattery. Beware associating with the devil, even in dreams. He's always the forerunner of despair and when pursued by his majesty, and you will fall into snares set by enemies in the guise of friends.*

Roya, sulking and taken aback, went back to bed. *It's been a long day with the kids.* Solomon was snoring and sleeping like a baby. *Something fishy is going on.* She longed for the answers. *Solomon departs without a trace, and no straight answer, either.* She slid under the covers, lying next to him, and stared at his face and saw his arm over the blanket getting his zees. His chest rises and descends. His breathing became quieter, peaceful rest. His handsomeness and sexiness spoke to her intellect as she licked her lips with a distasteful fantasy. Then, she slipped under the satin blanket. *Oh, that was a whooper jump. Calm down, little ones inside.* Roya rubbed her stomach, peering down at her plump belly to speak softly to her unborn children in her womb. *Tug of war inside. Kick here. Punch there. Ouch. That hurts.*

"What's wrong baby?" Solomon reached over and touched her belly gently. "Everything okay? Do we need to go?"

"No, Solomon. They're fine. Go back to sleep," she replied. Solomon then reached for Roya's hand to bring her closer to his warm body.

Solomon touched Roya's sensual spots that awakened her sexual appetite. He nodded his head seductively. Then he changed the mood by a sudden stop of satisfaction. *We lost this moment of any lovemaking. He needs to make time for love like the old days.* Roya cried in a whisper. Once they had kids, he works overtime, and there's no time for sex. *Dang, we haven't been intimate for a month. Business over pleasure. Solomon will jump to other business affairs rather than touch me, where I like.*

She glanced at his chest, so enticing and tempting while she stared at his 6-pack abs, hairless, and buff breasts. She slid next to him under the sheets. Solomon held Roya in his arms while kissing on her neck after moving her long, thick, curly hair out of the way. She shifted slightly. *My protruding pregnant stomach always gets in the way! I'll never do this again.* She kissed Solomon back on his lips. He responded with his eyes still closed. She wanted to go to sleep, but another part of her wanted him intimately. *If he keeps coming back with these small advances, I am going for the gold.* He yawned loudly. Solomon smacked his lips and dozed into dreamland.

Dang nab it! She whispered. She wanted Solomon to take her there. She pouted and unwrapped herself from his embrace and turned towards the end of the bed, looking at the window. Her eyelids became heavy. Eventually, she rolled back in the center of the king-size bed and fell back to sleep.

In the revelatory dream, she saw herself trapped in combat. War. Battle. Fire shoots from the sky. Tanks barrage unknown enemies as targets. Soldiers marching on the journey of doom as guns fired. Machine guns. Roya heard and watched tanks blast, fire in the sky. Men were falling to the ground from bombs exploding in the midst. *Who is that man in the midst? That's my father. He's rescuing a man from an explosion.* She watched the man's intestines gush out of his abdomen. *He's begging my father to kill him.*

"Please let me go to my maker," the cocoa-butter man mumbled from his lips as blood spewed. Foaming from the mouth, death appeared to be among his living soul.

"We have to make it back to the promised land," she heard. "My promised land is to be back at home to be with my wife and daughter. Roya is married, and she gave birth to twin boys. I still haven't seen my grandsons." She watched as Lazarus pulled a wallet from his back pocket and before he could dig out the picture, another soldier from his left side held a gun to his head.

The soldier spoke a language that was foreign to Lazarus as he stood with the gun aimed at his temple. Now the slender talky soldier was about to pull the trigger, but Lazarus prayed.

"Dear Heavenly Father, if it's your will, let it be done. I want to let my family know that I love them dearly. Please send your angels to let them know. Guide me and carry me to your kingdom." Roya watched as Lazarus tried to knock the gun out of the slender soldier's hand. His prayer was answered mysteriously. Lazarus wasn't shot as he checked his body. Another soldier whacked the back of a gun on Lazarus' head and dragged him about a half of mile back to their truck. He was brutally beaten by other Asian men inside the large truck. Hit with guns, fists from several men, kicked, and blood flew out of his mouth. He then was knocked out again by a pistol. Lazarus was blindfolded, so he would not know where he was dropped off. He was dressed in his uniform with his American stripes on his upper right soldier. *What was my father doing in China, if he was supposed to be fighting a war in Iraq? Maybe he was on a Special Operations mission.*

One of the heavier Chinese men was in charge and directing the men under his command to take Lazarus to an open cemented room with chains. The men chained Lazarus to the wall by his feet and hands. A Chinese man with great strength boldly lashed Lazarus' body with a whip until he could hardly speak.

"Stop." One of the Chinese men spoke in English and locked the room.

The men all walked away from the room. She saw his flesh hanging on his bones; his throat parched, and he looked like he had not eaten a meal in days. *Thirst.* Roya saw her father dying slowly from dehydration and blood dripping from his wounds, creating a dark red puddle. Screaming and wanting to rescue her father, not a finger could touch him since she was captured in this dream. Roya could only watch the brutality and feel his agony.

Lazarus coughed and gagged on his blood. He spoke in a whisper, "Heavenly Father, I pray that you will protect my family. I want to see my daughter fulfill her dreams. She's my little princess. Watch over my wife; I cannot envision any another man holding her and being with him. Let my daughter see her father as a hero. I'm ready to be a soldier in your army. Take me to your kingdom. I'm ready. Angels carry me. I love you, Jewel, and my other jewel, Roya."

He coughed up more blood. Then the Chinese men came back to throw water over his helpless bloody flesh. Lazarus was forced to drink dirty water. His body barely held on to life. He was taken from the chains and carried by three bulky men to their leader.

The Chinese leader questioned Lazarus about how many tanks, soldiers, and why they were fighting this war. *It is about power. It was world domination.* Lazarus nodded with the little energy he had in his body. He didn't flinch another muscle when the whip lashed.

"I'll tell you what you want to know if you allow me to live and to be with my family again," Lazarus begged.

"Promise," the Leader agreed.

"I hope this isn't the *kiss of death.*" Lazarus blurted.

"Sergeant Lazarus Battle. Is it really worth losing your life in a war that's unknown to your soldiers? You're only following commands, but you don't really understand the demands. In time you will know."

Roya suddenly found herself in the same room as her father and other captured men. The American soldiers were chained to the floor, hearing Asian men bickering and arguing behind the walls beneath. A television was on an American station while the former President was speaking about the attacks on China. Speaking in their dialect, only one Caucasian man on the top floor bond in chains could translate the message. He was the interpreter sent. Lazarus tried to break free from the shackles. He was combat-trained and found a kink in the chains. He regained his strength after a week of being fed some leftover slop usually fed to the animals. One of the Asian guards walked past, and her father kicked the Asian guard down to grab his weapon quickly. Lazarus broke the man's neck. *He is a hero.*

A cream sports car waited outside of the warehouse while the other soldiers surveyed the location since Lazarus was bugged. She watched as he was drafted and shipped over to the country, all the soldiers, including Lazarus, had a Verichip microchip inserted in his right hand. She listened as they were told it was a monitoring device to track all activities such as location, any sign of trouble and alert other secret service forces, or to report the death of a soldier to their families. He broke free to his escape. Machine guns ricocheting in his direction while some of the soldiers fired back on the field.

Roya pondered, *What the hell are we fighting for? Was it for power or world peace?*

One soldier sprinted to the vacant car, hotwired it, and sped off. Sergeant Lazarus made a run for it. Consequently, Lazarus was gunned down. Then other soldiers were blasted into the mid-air after walking over bombs. The explosions dismembered the military tanks and the soldiers. A bazooka targeted the cream sports car and fiery flames followed by grey smoke, flying ashes, and debris scattered through the air.

Roya awakened in a cold sweat. *Could this be true? Is this what really happened to people captured? What really happened to my father?*

Roya and Jewel never knew the truth. The military papers only indicated that Lazarus was dead. Yet, the military gave him a military funeral and handed Jewel the folded flag in honor of his death in war. Both women watched his casket being lowered into the ground. Guns held in the air blasted. Music played. They drove off in a limousine. *My daddy's body is on Iraq's soil.* Blowing kisses on the window shield, Roya wished she could see her father's smile. She remembered not hearing a single word Jewel or Solomon said on that day. *I wish I could see Daddy again. I loved his warmth, his hugs, and most of all, his kisses on my cheeks as if I was something sweet to eat.* Tears rolled down her cheeks.

Chapter 9

DNA on the Line

ROYA WHITMORE

Florida
Whitmore Mansion

Later that morning, Roya discovered a letter, from a sender she didn't recognize. She saw that it was addressed to her mother. "What's wrong, Mom?" Roya said.

Jewel seemed groggy and frowned at the question.

"Girl, please. Look at this letter I got at the post office." She shook it frantically in front of Roya.

"I went to check my mail before you woke up. Girl, you won't believe what is in this letter that I received. Well, I received two different letters that relate to each other," Jewel yelped.

"Calm down, first of all, you're talking so loud and fast, and I'm lost with what you're trying to convey. Please let me see the letters you're talking about since I'm clueless," Roya replied and held her hand out to review the paperwork.

"Here, Roya. I think I'm about to lose my dang old mind!" Jewel tapped her head.

"What! You mean you're just now getting the monies from the military for dad's death? That must be the letter I noticed earlier this morning." She pointed where it was sitting earlier, and Jewel nodded.

Roya changed gears, "Plus, dad died when I was twenty-three, which was about fourteen years ago. I know you received his pension, right? Since you were able to keep the house until now."

She was confused at her mother's sudden reaction. Jewel was a nervous wreck, shuffling paper, stomping her feet, and rampaging in the kitchen with disturbing news about going insane at 63. What did her mother mean about the two letters in her hands?

"Not exactly, I'm getting monies from his pension after his death, yes. However, this is a change in the claim for lesser monies since someone contacted them for child support. He's fathered, supposedly, two other children." Her voice lowered after her outburst, "I did have a child after you were born, about a year and a half later. I didn't tell your father either. I cheated on him. I wasn't sure if it was his child. Luckily I didn't show while he was home, but when he was stationed somewhere else for nine months. I had my child and gave her up for adoption. Your father came back home, even though he noticed I gained some weight, he never knew about the child. I didn't want to risk our marriage and family over an adulterous affair that didn't last past a week," wept Jewel.

Roya froze. "So, you mean that I have a *sister* that you never spoke of. Why now?"

"Roya, I think her adoptive parents are claiming some of his monies, too. And other baby mamas who want a piece of the pie! Can you believe this crap?" Jewel questioned.

Roya stared blankly and shook her head.

"I was worried about cheating on him once, and he's cheated a few times on me, but fathered these children. Correction: he produced other babies, but not a father to any of them. Ain't this a dang shame," Jewel snapped. She clapped her hands rigorously together on each syllable.

"Dang, mom. I don't know what to say. How many times have you grilled me on adultery and fornication? How you told me not to sleep around on my husband. I kept my cool and those legs closed, just as you said. You say, 'I'm so holier than thou,' now this drama from my own mama. So can they do this without a paternity test?" Roya wondered.

"Shoot. I don't know. Well, I read only some of it. It appears that they had requested a paternity test. They had to get his DNA from the grave and didn't ask my permission whatsoever. I believe it was some pathologist assigned to this case to match up the skeleton bones left behind, and reviews dental and medical records to find an exact match. You know the body decomposes, but the bones take much longer, sometimes centuries, I heard, before they dissolve to dust. That's what I get for watching the *Discovery* channel."

"Seriously, mom? Wow. You know all that?"

Jewel lightly shook her head and obviously was in deep thought before Roya interrupted her reverie.

"I thought they needed to find a relative of his to get the DNA that is needed for testing," Roya exclaimed.

"I guess they did ship his body back to the states. Apparently, they were able to prove this. My mind cannot contain the fact that there are others he fathered or some other women he impregnated while in the service."

Roya mouth fell agape.

"As for the fornication and adultery thing, I didn't want you to fall into this trap of deception like me. Mothers always want the best for their children and not to repeat their mistakes. Can you forgive me?" asked Jewel.

"No matter what, I love you and respect you. I know you want the best for me since I'm learning about all of this as a parent myself. Now, will you be able to survive off that check due to the changes? Also, I'm wondering if we can meet these siblings that are supposedly dad's seed. Do we know if they are male, or female? How about their ages?" Roya inquired.

"Good question. I'm not sure. I'll have to contact the person or office that drew up these papers. I want to make sure, instead of losing a grip of this pension check given to these other children, baby mama drama. Hold on, let me contact this office now," replied Jewel.

❋JOY WHITMORE❋

Despite their loud discussion, Joy had slept through it all. She rubbed the sleep out of her eyes and raced down the stairs. "What's for lunch, Mom? I'm hungry."

"You'll always be my princess, Joy, but you're getting old enough to fix lunch yourself," Roya said. "Go fix a sandwich. There are chips in the cupboard."

Joy responded, "Chips? You mean chips survived my bruhs?" She dashed to the cupboard.

❋ROYA❋

Roya shook her head and went upstairs. *Where is Solomon? I feel like things are going sour. I don't see him as often. Why doesn't he call me, or something? Oh well, maybe I've got a sister or a bunch.* Crazy. *Could Daddy go to hell for his sins? He did ask for God's help in my dream. Will I see him again in the kingdom of God—heaven?*

Jewel stormed in Roya's bedroom to bicker about the ordeal, "They'll have a court hearing. This way we can meet these mothers and the children to come to a conclusion on the payment situation. I don't want to live off of you and Solomon, but I'm wondering how I'll make these payments if the money has decreased and business ventures have slowed down."

"Mom, you'll just have to get a job. Back in the workforce, for a little while, I'm willing to help you. You just opened your business in Florida! That isn't doing as well, but you're doing well in Beverly Hills, California, right?"

"But, you and Solomon can take care of me." Jewel flashed a crooked smile.

"What!" Roya shot an outburst. Her eyes widened in shock at that statement.

"You are a writer, author, and actress. You are still living off the royalties of that best-selling book that also was a blockbuster hit fifteen years ago. Solomon is a music producer, actor, and working on lucrative projects. Why are you trying to play me? I'm your mother, remember? I paid for your college education, private schooling, and got your first car."

"Look, Mom; you got jokes." She chuckled. "This is my money that I worked so hard to get. I've got your grandchildren to take care of. You supported me to a certain extent, but I'm not obligated to take care of you. You were obligated to take care of me until I turned eighteen, and then my wings flew out of your hairs shortly after that. You're grown, Ma. You can manage. I allowed you to come and visit, to assist me, but I thought I was your only child. So, what are you going to do about the child that you gave up for adoption?" Roya wondered with a twinge of anger in her voice.

"Oh, so it's like that. Dang. I feel crushed. Kids are a trip. Then, you have three and on number four. You turned on me like this. Boy, we take care of yaw and yaw turn your backs on parents when we need you the most." She ignored Roya's question and dragged out the issue about these illegitimate children.

"Oh boy. Mom, calm down. I don't mind, but I also have to check with my husband. Chill." Roya patted her shoulder. "I was just saying. We don't owe you anything."

She reiterated. "I'm willing to help, but don't expect it just like you were living off dad's check. I cannot believe my father was like that. I dreamed about him the other night."

"What? You did? What was it about?" Jewel leaned closer to hear the dream.

"Him fighting some war. Dad was fighting and rescuing another soldier until he was captured and tortured. He then rescued other soldiers from this warehouse and then was gunned down. Bombs exploded, destroying everything in sight. Crazy, huh?" Roya's eyebrows furrowed, and she tapped on the counter.

"Not really. From what I read in the papers and overheard, this is what happened to your father. Maybe not so much in detail as you dreamed, but pretty close." Jewel's eyes glistened.

"Wow." Roya screeched.

"Whoa. You're getting revelations like that! I know the Bible speaks of how man will dream dreams. Lord knows, I named you right!" Jewell said ecstatically.

Roya changed the subject. "So, when's the court date?"

"Here, this is the date. How do you feel about all this?" Jewel wondered. She handed the court typed-letter to her to review.

"I'd like to meet my sister that you had shortly after my birth. How do you feel about that?" Roya asked.

"I'm curious who Lazarus cheated with and if they're really your father's children. I'd love to see ourselves on the Maury show. First, we dealt with President Bush that had something to do with power and oil issue back in 2001 with

Iraq, when your father fought a war uncalled for." Jewel rattled on.

"So, was my father in this war back in the day and he died?" Roya scratched her head.

"I believe it was when you were twenty-three or four, I think. This was a secret war while President George W. Bush was in office his second term. We're blessed, finally, to make history with President Barack Obama in office and made it as long as he has, girl! I believe this is the year of the deceiver to come into office." Jewel spoke in circles.

Roya's mouth was agape, and her eyes bulged at the words. She just had nightmares about the devil, Satan himself. She thought about her mother's words, *year of the deceiver* and *into office. An Antichrist is coming into office, presidential office, soon.*

"However, I'm still tripping that your father cheated. But, in a way, can I blame him? He'd be gone for months at a time. That is why I was tempted to cheat. He was gone too dang old long for me. A woman has needs, same as a man. But, it doesn't excuse us from God's commandments for our lives. We both were wrong."

"I feel ya." Roya agreed.

Chapter 10

New Tracking Measures

SOLOMON WHITMORE

Florida
Saved Disciples Association

Solomon conducted a meeting with a live presentation on a virtual conference call. "We're transitioning from sliding credit cards, showing our driver license, eliminating bank cards and work ID cards, even leisure cards to biometric chips that will be implanted in our bodies to detect our every move. In other words, it's a tracking device that monitors everything we do, buy, and sell. Our world is subject to a soft tyranny of omniscient and interlocking regimes of control." He sipped on his water.

"Work rules overlap with criminal law, which overlaps with official morals, and those overlap with concerns of security, political polices, and problematic assumptions with our government. We moved from visual surveillance, also known as closed-circuit television (CCTV), to satellite cameras on our streets, parks, doorways, and freeways. For instance, in the U.K. alone, there are millions of cameras nationwide to watch train stations, buildings, shops, and other public places. We have been infiltrated here in U.S. too. Already, there are over two point five million

Americans that are implanted with a microchip; their identity is read by handheld scanners in grocery stores, local shops, and now even at the gas stations. Can you believe this!" He spoke without catching his breath.

"Listen, there is constant surveillance forced on loyal citizens, trained soldiers, obedient patients in hospitals concerned about their medical conditions and now, our productive workers by replacing their badges and work cards! This is their bio-power! They have power over our lives as if they're God." He licked his lips.

"Discipline increases utility and diminishes obedience. Our souls are imprisoned in the body since these devices are able to record, store, and track our movements. Surveillance infrastructure of colonial America began here, "memorandum born," in which we were simple accounts of human lives under the slave master— the government and their constant new laws, and we must abide by their rules and regulations or else!" He paused to glance over his notes. He wanted to make sure he wasn't missing any details. The *street disciples* needed to know what they were up against in this *new* world.

"Eventually, we'll be unable to escape the implantation of these devices in our bodies. There will be no more freedoms of speech, religion, or anything else. This has been going on for more than a decade. They started with animals, then military and the sickly. Now they are moving to us— regular civilians." He rose from his seat, pumping his fist. "Men, we have to stand up! We have to fight and orient our families to the new generation. Will we take the mark? Or will we take the seal of God?" His voice elevated to a yell.

Several people had questions. If they became too difficult to answer, Solomon would hand them over to the CEO, Isaiah Ezekiel Williams.

"I'd love to add, and answer your question about the slave master; we can look back at 1840's publishers producing ledgers. Producing ledgers for plantation management, to keep track of their slaves on the plantation, called the "Cotton Plantation Record and Account Book, No. 1 Suitable for a Force of 40 Hands or Under." Isaiah gave a brief history lesson where this all took place, letting the followers know that *history repeats itself.*

"This was a written surveillance system of slaves, for instance, those given slave passes. There were organized slave patrols to chase down slaves that escaped from the plantation, and placed up wanted posters for runaways and used them as another way to control them. Dixie invented the slave patrols. There was also surveillance and corporal punishment, by which patrollers empowered other citizens to search homes for runaways, weapons, or escape plans. This will take place in our laws today through technical devices and martial law." He exclaimed with enthusiasm.

"According to history accounts, Charleston, South Carolina in 1783, adopted tamper-proof technology, a system of metal "slave tags" or "slave hire badges." And today it is microchips in our hands, similar to a barcode on items we buy in stores, to scan and read off information on a person such a birthplace, bank account information, etcetera." He then held up the book where he got these accounts from and explained for the others to, "Read more on biometrics in books like *The Soft Cage: Surveillance in America from Slave Passes to the War on Terror* and *Lockdown America*."

Isaiah added, "In that time, fugitives were credited to new identities, and we have to follow this same format. We're finding new ways to change and hack into systems to change our identities! This was a method used in restraint and surveillance tactics. History repeats itself since we have surveillance cameras plugged everywhere, but now the new tactic is implanted in your body."

Solomon read the comment sent through chat and spoke in the microphone for the video conferencing. "To answer your question, sir, we've hacked into their computer systems and have others that work in the CIA, FBI, and other tracking/surveillance offices to ensure that we're not being recorded on one of these small cameras in the district. We also are recording this meeting, and it can be uploaded on your satellites, computers, and other electronic devices to inform others; however, you have to convert your phones by taking them to our deactivation center to make sure it's not being traced!"

Isaiah went back to the subject at hand, "Mark of the Beast, man-made number 666, isn't necessarily this chip in our right hand or head; yet the Bible speaks about being in our hands or minds. In other words, we're following the worldly system to buy or sell! Some will cry, and ask God to forgive them. 'I had to feed my family. I had to work to provide for my family.' In our society, people allow their

✝ 89

mindsets to follow the world instead of God's Word, which symbolizes the mark being in our head and following others refers to the mark being in our hand. I could elaborate more on this topic, but our time has expired. We've gone a few minutes over, and we need to depart at this time. Would someone like to lead us in prayer?"

Someone lead the prayer session, shortly later, most of the men departed out of the facility and those online signed out. A few stayed to speak to Solomon or Isaiah to find out more about this private organization.

Isaiah was a jovial character. He took a brief second, to explain why his mother named him after two prophets in the Bible, Isaiah and Ezekiel. His first name is Isaiah, and middle name is Ezekiel. So he decided to name his sons the names separately, his first born Isaiah Jr. and second son, Ekiel pronounced E-kee-el.

Solomon learned that Isaiah is a multicultural individual, being part African and Italian, as his mother was English and Irish. Isaiah was fairly light-skinned with piercing green eyes. He stood five feet ten inches, lean, and slightly muscular. He was in the military for twenty years, and fluently speaks Italian, Spanish, and Irish and English dialect because of his family members traveled around the country and while he was in the military. Later, Isaiah was a born-again Christian and joined the Seventh Day Adventists.

Now Isaiah's mission was to teach others and share the gospel regardless of character, background, race, or religion and Solomon joined the organization. It wasn't about religion, but the teachings of the gospel and discovering the truth in God's Holy Word. Isaiah was noted for creating the organization called Alliance of Crusaders for Christ since the world was lost, especially now this new world system was capturing the minds of men and women. Although no one knows the time or hour of Jesus Christ return (Second Coming of Christ), there is more and more evidence that the last days are near.

Solomon joined Alliance of Crusaders for Christ after attending at a Seventh Day Adventist church on a sermon called *Revelation is Nearer than you Think*! Even if Solomon's wife and family attended a Seventh Day Adventist church, he was skeptical about this religion since he grew up as a Baptist. But Solomon never learned so much in his life and realized that he's not about religion, but seeking and knowing the truth. *A small lie can turn into the whole truth, and this is how the Antichrist will deceive others.*

These meetings are conducted by only males until we feel it is safe to wives and invite women. Furthermore, Alliance Crusaders for Christ was originated to get men prepared for the Mark of the Beast. Our mission was to save canned food, and store clothing in warehouses and other secret buildings for when one is unable to buy and sell unless they have the mark 666. Those buildings are technology-equipped with computer software and hardware to assemble and operate when this moment strikes.

These missions were accomplished after reading scriptures from the book of Genesis chapter forty-one, Joseph's story in Egypt when he had to interpret Pharaoh's dream. The dream was about the seven cows and seven heads of grain, which Joseph let Pharaoh understand what the dream meant: seven years of plenty and seven years of drought. These men were preparing for the seven years' reign of the Antichrist controlled by Satan. Many will be unable to survive the "drought" after the peace treaty is broken—three and half years from now.

Watch and pray. There have been various signs for centuries that make people become worried about the Antichrist. People even started to worry about Jesus returning to gather up His saints after watching movies that warned them to get ready for when the Antichrist will strike.

I want to tell Roya about the Alliance Crusaders for Christ. She'll probably blow it out of proportion—throw it up in my face and laugh. I don't want to alarm her unless it's absolutely necessary. He also visualized Roya as a devoted soldier in the battle, because of her sincere love for Christ.

❀SOLOMON❀

After the meeting, Solomon drove home with his wife on his mind. He looked at the smaller trees swaying left and right from the effects of the wind. Solomon pulled up in the garage and unlocked the door to get inside the home. No one was home. *What a day. I want to feel the water rinsing me off and making me squeaky clean.*

Afterward, he sprayed on some Sean John body cologne and turned on the television while lying in the king-size bed. *No kids: quiet and relaxing. No wife nagging or asking questions. No mother-in-law. Before turning off the ringer, the phone rang.*

"Hello."

"Hello. Oh, so you are home?"

"Yea. How are you, Roya?"

"I'm okay. I miss you. I was worried about you."

"I love you too. I miss you too. Since no one was here, I took a shower and tried to unwind. Then the phone rang. I was dreaming about you."

"Don't make me laugh. Seriously, quit playing," Roya said, with a twinge of annoyance.

"Anyways, where are you?"

"I'm in the grocery store and the kids are at the park with Mom. So, how are you? And yes, I'd like to hear this so-called message I left, you know, that's your mistress!" She teased.

Solomon snapped, "What the heck? I almost slipped and cursed, but you're tripping."

He paused to gather his thoughts and carefully choose his words, "Remember this: you are the only woman I love, and my body belongs to Roya. I hope that's Roya on the other end of the receiver."

Roya did not respond.

Then he used his most monotonic voice, "Hello. Calling Roya. Roya are you there?"

"Ha. Ha. Ha. Funny. Wait until I get home," she said. "I. Will. Break. You, off."

"Oh really? Okay," Solomon chanted. "Holla at me later," Roya hung up the phone before Solomon could say another word.

Whitmore Mansion

Solomon turned the television off and fell asleep. He dreamed about the life of Joseph. He watched Potiphar's wife asking Joseph, "Lie with me." She was engrossed by Joseph's handsome face and body and obviously desired being touched by him intimately. Solomon saw Joseph refusing his master's wife. It was a sin against God. Not only did Joseph refuse Potiphar's wife advances, but he ran. Later, Joseph was thrown in prison for two years, and then Solomon's dream fast forwarded to Pharaoh's dream and how Joseph interpreted it. Then, Joseph became a leader over the food supply known as Zaphnath-Paaneah.

Solomon knew this was a revelation from God. He stored canned goods, survival tools, and camping equipment for those who refuse to take the mark of the Antichrist. He also instilled survival skills before the war of persecution of Christians. Although there were other Antichrists in King Solomon's time and in the past like Hitler and Charles Manson, he knew, without a doubt, that this biochip would be the harbinger of the times to come.

He was awakened by the laughter of his children, wife's voice in the other room, and his mother-in-law responding. Roya entered in the room, seeing him waking up while twisting and turning in the bed. She closed the door behind her, locking it. She quickly undressed, hoping Solomon would explore her body. He moved closer to Roya, tasting and pleasing his wife intimately. She was well-satisfied by the sounds that came from her lips and facial expressions of ecstasy. *She's mine!*

Chapter 11
Birth Pangs

ROYA WHITMORE

Florida
Whitmore Mansion

Roya woke up in the middle of the night with sharp pains in her lower abdomen. She shrieked at the abrupt, intense pain surging through the side of her stomach. Solomon awakened in alarm when he heard her second shriek; this time more aggressive and slightly lower than a scream.

He groggily said, "Baby...is that you?"

She panted, "Uh-huh."

"Is it time?" He turned to her side, touching her lower abdomen.

She felt his semi-circular motion as taught in the pre-and-post natal classes. He pressed gently across again and again in hopes to ease her contraction. "Breathe, Roya," he said. She calmed, practicing her breathing and relaxing as they had learned.

He leaned closer and sat against the headboard on his side.

"How are you feeling now?" He reached to the two-drawer dresser for his watch.

She watched him look at the dials on the watch. She knew he was timing the contractions.

"So I take it that contraction happened around 2:19 a.m." He said calmly and low to nearly a whisper.

She lightly shook her head in agreement. She then closed her eyes for a moment to recollect her thoughts on previous pregnancies and labor to delivery experiences. The minutes were ticking away, but she glanced at his face in the dim lighting from the night lights scattered in the room. He seemed confused and curious at the same time.

"Why the *face*?" She teased.

"What *face*?" He spoke in a serious tone.

"Um...that one on your face now. Your head slightly tilted to the side and got that confused but thoughtful look." She pointed and then touched his chin. She cupped his chin in her palm.

"Just in deep thought, I guess." He sighed. "I love you so much. I hope this childbirth goes well. I fear of losing you but know we serve a God that can perform miracles if we just believe. So I believe he would not give me you, these children, to only lose the good woman he has given me." His voice lowered and wavered.

She lightly slapped her palms across his muscular cheeks. She pursued her lips. "Don't even think that way. Shake that thought away." She curved a smile. "I love you more than words could express." She reached for his hand and laid it on the lower part to the right side of her abdomen. The contractions returned more aggressively.

"I take that was another one." He rose and sat upright.

She nodded. She squeezed her hands tightly as if her nails were clawing for blood.

"No need to squeeze your hands. Just breathe. Like this," He took long breaths. He instructed, "In and out. Yes, baby, you got this."

"Stop it."

"What?" He shrugged in confusion.

"That look." She fussed.

"This..." He casted 'the look' purposely. "And look at this," He stuck out his tongue to change her disposition. Her frown turned into a slight smile. She hissed with a giggle.

"Just get ready to take me to the hospital." She shooed him to the living room for the travel size suitcase on wheels.

"Don't your contractions have to be closer?" He asked, jumping out of the bed.

"Well, that was the second one about ten minutes apart. So you better call the doctor too. Oh! And my mom! I want her to be there in the delivery room with us."

"You sure, Roy?" He inquired, and he pouted.

"Ugh. I want my mother in the room! I hate when you call me Roy!" She snapped. She turned on the side of the bed, slipped her feet into the slippers below, and stood up with her hands on her hips.

"Ok, Ro-Ro let me go, go." He joked and exited the room.

"I know you are getting the suitcase!" She yelled then felt another contraction. She doubled over. She quickly lifted up, worried about putting pressure and stress on the unborn child. She stumbled to the threshold. She held on the sides of the threshold before stepping in the hallway.

She took a few more steps to the stairwell. She felt a burst of water running down her thighs to her feet. She felt a puddle of water on her toes. She shouted, "My water broke!"

She panted. She lifted her head upwards and whispered, "I'm only seven months and three weeks." She mused on what her doctor had said at her most recent check-up. *The baby can come two weeks early or late.* She shook her hands. "No way." She blurted, "I still have almost two months, not two weeks...all my other babies came near the due dates."

She didn't know that Solomon was eavesdropping. "Lord Jesus, it is going to be alright." She hummed a song to calm her spirit and shake away the worries. "I put my worries on the altar."

Solomon fast walked around the corner and jogged up the stairs. "It's going to be alright, Roya." He reached forward to assist.

In the past, Roya had pleaded with Solomon to get a vasectomy. She had to shake that negative thought while the contractions became more intense and frequent. He glanced at his watch again. "They are even closer. I called the doctor while getting your bag out of the living room closet."

"Did you...," Roya gasped between breaths, "call momma?"

He heard her labored breathing. He demanded, "Roya, breathe. Slowly." He practiced the breaths with her. "Remember what they told us in class?"

She continued with long, heavier pants.

"Breathe. Like this." He coached. "Okay, Roya, let's get you to the hospital."

He carefully assisted her down each stair at her pace. Once they reached the bottom stair, he released his hands and grabbed the overnight travel bag on wheels. Then he turned to let her lean on him. She wrapped her right arm behind his neck. His freehand rolled the travel bag across the floor and through the door to the car while holding her on his other side as she took steps in slow motion.

Blood trickled down Roya's legs as he raced to place the bag in the trunk, then opened her door, and helped her inside. He pushed the engine start button.

He saw red splotches on her white nightgown before she sat inside. "Roya, you're bleeding," he said as he searched to see the blood coming from underneath her gown, down her legs.

"No. My water broke while I was upstairs." She exclaimed and breathed.

Cradling Roya, he cried out to Jesus, "Jesus, please let my baby be healthy. In Jesus' Name, I pray, Amen."

The ambulance siren roared as it came nearer to their home.

"Is that the ambulance?" She asked frantically.

He nodded in agreement. "I called."

"Do you want me to drive you to the hospital?" He asked.

"Why would you do that, *silly,* if they are coming here?" She shooed him and waved her hand at him to shoot down that impractical suggestion.

He opened his car door and hopped from the driver's seat to race to the passenger side. He quickly opened the door to escort her outside. Crying and praying to God, Solomon attempted to comfort her and joined in prayer. "Lord, please keep your hand over *our* babies," she cried.

"God has you covered," Solomon reassured her. "He would never leave you or forsake you." He whispered as the sirens blared.

Paramedics raced to Roya and then wheeled her to the ambulance van. She was lifted on a stretcher while a paramedic checked and read her vital signs.

"Can I come with you?" Solomon inquired loudly.

The man flagged him to come inside. He climbed inside, next to his wife's left side. He touched her hand and clasped hers into his. "She doesn't need to be induced. Her water broke already, but we are concerned about the blood."

"Where?" the paramedic asked. He tilted his head and then cut the gown upward.

"Was that necessary?" Solomon quizzed. "You could have just lifted her gown without cutting it."

The paramedic didn't answer. He called her current condition in to the hospital and confirmed she'd be delivering the babies. After checking with Solomon, he gave the doctor's name and midwife that would be in the room during the childbirth.

Solomon had a concerned look about delivering the babies early.

The paramedic sympathized, "She'll be fine. Sometimes bleeding does occur. This is not her first child, right?"

"Nope. The last child." Solomon answered, looking to Roya for approval.

Since they had put an oxygen mask over her nose and mouth, she blinked her eyes in agreement. Her pain was intense and grew every few minutes. She squeezed her eyes tighter. Solomon leaned over and rubbed her shoulder.

"I'm here. Wait. We are here, already."

She felt the abrupt stop. She heard the engine still running. The paramedic pushed the van doors open. The driver raced around to the back of the van to assist with pulling the stretcher out. Solomon jumped out before they proceeded. The stretcher unfolded to the pavement, and they all rushed through the hospital emergency doors. Solomon kept up with their pace while holding his wife's hand. She squeezed tighter when another contraction happened.

"Whoa!" He screeched. "That was an intense one...that hurt!" He released his hand for a brief moment and shook it.

Her face tightened. Her skin color turned pinkish-red. Her eyes tightened, seeing the lines form. A line creased her forehead. Her cheeks became rosy red. She pushed her breath. She inhaled, intensely. Her lips were cracked.

She heard her doctor's voice, "Come this way." She motioned the paramedics.

The nurses and midwife raced towards them and took it from there. Roya was lifted from the stretcher to theirs. They quickly wheeled Roya into the delivery room. Solomon didn't leave her side.

"Thankful you are here." He directed his comment to the midwife and doctor. Roya smiled, slightly, when she saw her husband there.

"Where's mom? You called her, right?" She mumbled, hurriedly.

"She will be here shortly. Promise." He rubbed her hand and then moved up her arm gently. The hairs on her arms rose.

"You have goose bumps. Are you cold?" He asked once they propped her bed at a 45 angle.

She shook her head no.

"Okay, I got your blanket that you so love," He added, gently placing it over her chest. He teased her with his eyes.

She couldn't help but chuckle lightly.

She was positioned to push.

"Solomon, I need to speak to Roya alone for a moment." The doctor requested him to stand outside for a moment.

He turned to walk towards the door.

Roya screamed, "I will not deliver this baby without my husband in the room! Ooh!"

He froze and didn't move until directed by the doctor.

"There are some things I need to discuss with you before delivering these babies. Does he even know you are carrying twins?" She questioned, and eyes darted at Roya then to Solomon.

"No." Roya shook her head.

"Why didn't you tell me, Roy?" Solomon exclaimed with a twinge of anger as he traipsed.

"You've been terribly busy." She threw her hands up. "And he missed some of the ultrasounds and appointments." She excused him.

"I do not want to put any stress on these babies." The doctor stressed. "This is high risk childbirth since you have high blood pressure and we may have to proceed with a cesarean. I also considered your age since you are over 35."

"Je—us!" She wailed.

"We need to get her in this." The doctor directed the nurse to handle the gown.

Solomon sat nearby. He then rose from his seat to question the doctor. "Will I be able to stay in the room if she gets the C-section?"

"If we have no serious complications and quickly have to proceed, then you are welcome to stay."

"Does she have serious complications?" He questioned with concern.

"Let me see if the membranes rupture without the onset of labor."

"English, please? Layman terms." Solomon exclaimed.

"She bled right?"

"Correct."

"After her water broke, it appears that her membranes ruptured without any labor contractions."

"I think she had contractions because she woke me up with her agonizing shrieking."

"How many contractions did you witness?"

"Definitely two or three."

"Which one? Two or three?" She rose up two fingers on one hand and three on the other.

"Two," Solomon answered quickly.

"How far apart?"

"I would say ten minutes. After the first two, I called you."

"Ok," She tapped her chin with her forefinger.

Solomon stood by her right side as the doctors speedily setup and propped her feet up for delivery. A nurse wheeled an IV bag next to her bed. She appeared drowsy from the first insertion of a needle in her right hand. He watched the drips of anesthesia come from the bag through the thin tube to her hand.

"We need to get her prepped. Turn her on her side and start the epidural block."

The midwife injected, "Shouldn't we wait until she dilates a little more?"

"I have examined her vagina and see she has dilated five centimeters. But with her being a high risk candidate already because of her age, high blood pressure, and bleeding before delivering..."

"I believe we should wait." The midwife countered.

"Let's check the babies' heart rate. We need to insert the fetal monitor inside to see the babies' heart rate." The doctor demanded.

"Hold on, Doctor. I see her temperature according to the mother's monitors show her temperature rose past 100.5. She's up to 103." The nurse prepared the fetal heart monitor.

Solomon glanced at the monitors. He studied them carefully. He then held his wife's hand. He knew he could not comfort her during the anguish. He only knew to coach her and encourage her during the contractions.

"So what is going to happen, Doc Turner?" Solomon asked cautiously. "After the readings, I see the nurse and midwife stepped out. Is that protocol?"

"We are preparing for a blood transfusion and taking all precautions. I want the best for my patient and the children coming forth. We discussed this Roya, right?" Dr. Turner sounded assuring.

Roya nodded lightly. The other nurse checked the ultrasound wave patterns read on the paper running down to the floor. The midwife and nurse reentered the room.

Dr. Turner pulled vinyl gloves on her hands. She directed the nurse to shave the area.

She motioned Solomon to go in the top drawer to get the basin. His eyes glared confusion. He obeyed her order.

"Why am I bleeding, doctor?"

"It could be a vaginal tear," Doctor replied. Her tone shifted. "Right now, it is more important to make sure the delivery of your child goes well. But I'm not clear yet why you're bleeding. Did it happen directly after the water breaking?"

"Yes. I believe it did happen a little later." Roya exclaimed.

"Please let us know, Dr. Turner," said Solomon, holding Roya's hand tightly.

"Her blood pressure rose a bit, but it is to be expected." The midwife offered.

"Put the basin near her mouth." She raised her hand as if she was putting the basin under Roya's mouth.

"Why?" he asked, and seconds later she vomited. "Whoa. How did you know?"

"She is obviously nauseous, and I've been doing this quite a long time. I saw the look." Dr. Turner answered.

"Her other vital signs are okay at this moment. But we want to see your blood pressure go down a bit. More importantly, we want to deliver your children." She affirmed.

The door swung open. "I hope I am not too late."

"Mom! You made it." She smiled. "Where or who is watching the kids?"

"I was going to bring them with me when I stopped at the house. But in the fridge, you had the next door neighbor's number marked in red under the emergency numbers reading 'babysitter on call.' So I called, and she came over quickly to watch them for me. Well for you." She explained.

The midwife helped with the barring down stage. She exclaimed to try to have a natural birth instead of the C-section.

"Roya. I know you wanted the midwife present to be comfortable in the hospital setting, but I think it is best to prepare for the cesarean. This is not a time to waver."

"Dr. Turner is right," Roya said.

Solomon passed an ice chip after the nurse wheeled the cart nearby him. He placed a wet towel on her forehead while she took gentle breaths.

"I checked her again. She has dilated about another centimeter in the past thirty minutes. Her breathing is becoming longer. She's taking shallow breaths, meaning the contractions are more intense and closer. Keep monitoring her. I will return," Dr. Turner said.

"Where is she going?" Jewel inquired.

"She is getting ready for the C-section. She'll be back soon. Roya, I want you to focus on your breaths. Proceed, Solomon, with the rubbing of her stomach in a semi-circular motion to ease her contractions." The midwife commanded.

❊SOLOMON❊

Solomon rubbed. He watched his wife's scrunched nose, squeezed eyes, and face tighten then relax to a slowly softened face. She took stronger and shorter breaths. "Yes. Take shorter breaths like this." He took two shallow breaths and then two short breaths. He did two breaths in and two breaths out. She repeated.

He lifted the bed and lifted her to fluff the pillow. He noticed the red button "PUSH IF assistance is needed," and reached into his pocket for his phone. The phone vibrated. He ignored the call he saw flash across the screen.

"You still want me to record their birth?" He glared into his wife's eyes with compassion.

She lifted her head up and down slowly. He wasn't sure if it was an indication of labor pain from the strong contractions or a definite yes to his question.

"Roya. They want to do a C-section with this baby." Jewel said with a slight tinge of fear in her voice.

"Correction. Babies. She is having twins." Solomon expressed.

"Yes, mom. I am high risk with age, high blood pressure, and vaginal bleeding after the water broke," Roya explained.

"Glad mommy is here." Jewel's voice sounded like she was coming to the rescue.

"Glad I was able to reach you," Solomon added. "I called you right after calling the doctor."

"Oh, good. So you did call Mommy after the doctor," Roya repeated as if she sounded unsure.

"Remember? In the room, you said, 'call my doctor and oh, my mom." He imitated in her desperation voice.

He recorded her reaction after his mimicking as she waved him to get away from her. He chuckled. Jewel sat next to her and rubbed her arm then planted a kiss on her forehead. "Baby Girl, Mommy is here."

Dr. Turner returned in a green cloth gown tied in the back. Solomon still saw her white coat and black pants through the tied gown in the back. He recorded at a distance. Dr. Turner crouched down and sat on the rolling stool. The nurses quickly turned Roya on her side. Jewel was escorted by the midwife to leave the room. Jewel pleaded to stay in the room, but only the father was able to stay. Solomon carefully watched the epidural being injected in his wife's back. He first saw the smaller needle to inject the anesthesia around the back area.

"So you are making those small injects to numb her back?" Solomon inquired.

"Yes." The doctor answered.

"We request you to stop recording during the epidural block. You are allowed on the doctor's request and approval ahead of time for the childbirth experience." The nurse spoke and motioned him to put the phone away.

The midwife quietly coached Roya.

Solomon obeyed without questioning.

"This will take 15 minutes. Let us know how you are doing, Roya," The nurse asked after making another injection in another area near the small of her back.

She grunted. "Okay."

"After the conduction anesthetic in the lower area of the back, use the hypodermic needle. She will get repeated doses of the anesthesia." The doctor said calmly. "Now you may not feel the urge to push because of the epidural, but I will instruct you when to push." Her eyes reassured her with her calming voice.

Solomon raced to his wife's side. "Two panting breaths in and two blowing breaths out."

She nodded in agreement and obeyed. She took shallow breaths with her lips slightly parted. Her breaths became gentle and rhythmically.

"I love you." He said caringly.

"Ditto."

The nurse followed the orders given by the doctor. Solomon's eyes bulged upon seeing the larger hollow needle. She then placed a green-like sheet over Roya's legs. Her hospital gown was lifted up to her breasts. The green squared cloths lay at all four sides circumvented around the pregnant belly. The yellow antiseptic dabbed and rubbed her belly.

Then, he videotaped the following procedure in preparation for the cesarean on his Galaxy note. She was laid flat on her back now. The doctor motioned him to go on the other side of the green sheet hung across her belly. He stood near the upper half of her body, seeing her face, chest, and upper part of the stomach. Her eyes cried for him to be near. He read the cue. He held the phone while saying, "I'm here. Mom is here." He added for comfort. "You can do this, baby."

A lone tear ran down the side of his eye. He sniffled.

"Can my mom come in the room, please?" Roya pleaded.

"Not a good idea." The doctor advised.

"I need her for support," Roya exclaimed.

"I'm here, baby," Solomon said.

"I want my mommy, too."

The doctor saw her blood pressure spike. She motioned the nurse to get the mother.

"Ignoring visiting regulations. Let the mother in."

Solomon noticed the mother at the door, seeing her through the rectangular window on the door. The doctor motioned her to come in.

She stormed in the room, "Where's something to wipe my daughter's head!" She was handed a wet cloth by the nurse who escorted her in. She dabbed it gently on Roya's forehead. Solomon rubbed Roya's shoulder then arms.

"Doctor, how's *she* doing?" Jewel whined.

Solomon sensed an emotional, irate mother, continually wiping the sweat from her daughter's face and then planting another kiss.

❁ROYA❁

Roya envisioned pushing the children out while her mother encouraged her to push with the doctor. But the glimpse of reality was over—the tearing of the lower abdomen was done. She saw the first baby raised in the air and over the green cloth separating her lower half. The baby was quickly placed in a waiting incubator next to them. Solomon drew closer and lowered to his wife's head as they stared at the baby.

"Beautiful. You did *good*." Solomon said.

"Aww, my grandchild." Jewel cried.

"Boy," The nurse announced.

The next baby was taken out and lifted to view after putting a suction tube in the mouth and nose of the infants.

"Girl."

"Oh, Lord," Roya sighed. Sweat dripped from every inch of her body, clothes soaked from the perspiration. Drips of sweat tapped on her tongue. The salty, musty taste prickled her taste buds.

The doctor clamped the lifeline, umbilical cord, to cut from the second child delivered. She quickly stitched Roya's abdomen. Roya felt discomfort with the pulling of the stitches. The babies were cleaned and measured. While Solomon and Jewel observed the babies being fully examined, Roya felt the urge to push out the placenta and told the nurse. Dr. Turner took a blood sample before removal of the afterbirth. Dr. Turner then instructed her to push, catching the afterbirth in a metal basin.

Chapter 12

Darkness on my Soul

ROYA WHITMORE

Florida
Hospital

Roya passed out. Darkness filled her eyes. She no longer heard the voices of Dr. Turner, midwife, nurse, and nurse assistant. The cheers and encouragement of Solomon and Jewel faded away.

She fulfilled the prophecy of having five children as God had told her. Fourteen years ago, when she was twenty-three years old, God spoke to her spirit that she would have five children after marriage. She didn't believe God's will for her life and didn't intend for it to come true. Now, she was the mother of another set of twins—five children in the house!

She stared at a Southern two-story mansion home, antique white siding and black shutters, and wraparound porch. She didn't see her husband. Then she transported in the backyard, noticing a basket near her foot beneath a stringy clothesline. She drew nearer to the clothes hanging on the line, swaying back and forth from the gusty winds. The line hung from one tree to the other end. She heard crunching sounds as she stepped over the leaves blanketing the grass. She quickly took the dry clothing down and placed the clothes in the basket. Then she kneeled down to the ground, looking at the sky, and saw the skies become a dusky gray.

Oddly, she became aware of gravesites. She stared at four tombstones lying near the oak trees. She noticed her grandfather's tombstone, Sunnie Joe Betts, engraved on the tombstone, next to his wife's tombstone, Essie May, and her mother's grandmother, Willene Hill and was unable to make out the fourth one. She assumed it was her paternal grandfather, Clementon Battle, who was called Clem and had passed the following year.

The wind howled and blew so strongly that her basket flew over the grass. She felt the sting as leaves were blown in her face. She knew that gray skies usually meant rain or a storm was coming. She smelled the rain. The clouds were no longer bright and calm. Roya felt sad at the thought of losing her grandparents, having seen their deaths before it transpired.

She rushed to the backdoor of the home. As she came close to the doorstep, she saw the clouds go dark. Lightning and thunder followed. She stopped. "Wait," she thought. "That's not thunder. It sounds more like chariots of horses trampling. Like hundreds." She stood, frozen. She looked up. A demon-like creature was appearing in the sky. "Boy," she thought. "That thing is hideous." The wind forced her backwards, and she was unable to move any further. She saw herself glaring strangely at an abnormal voluminous image storming through the winds as the sounds of horses galloping grew louder. She looked around. No horses. The creature's wings flapped harder and faster towards her. As he flew through the clouds, she glanced at his hardened facial expressions. On his chest, he was wearing armor made of a steel breastplate reminding her of the past battles fought in ancient times. His arms were buff, with a muscular stature like a bodybuilder. His scorpion-like tail whipped, and lashed out at her, and stung her as she waved her hands feverishly to get through the fierce winds to turn the knob on the side door. She ran up the stairs quickly while holding her left hip where the beast inflicted pain. She met Jewel at the door, wondering what was wrong.

"What's going on? You act like you saw something that scared you to death! Your son's sleeping. I made your bath water to relax in."

"Thanks, Mom. I might be seeing things. I made it inside before the storm. He stung me, right here!" She pointed at the wound.

"What the heck are you talking about girl? Girl, go take your bath in Epson salt and Witch Hazel to avoid that wound getting infected. Unwind. I'll finish cooking dinner, come join us after your bath." Jewel advised.

Roya nodded. She saw other young women sitting at the dining table. She assumed these beautiful ladies were from her father's adulterous activities while traveling to countries on secret missions before his death in Iraq. She acknowledged her adopted sister because she favored their mother. No doubt in her mind, it had to be her. Jewel called her Sunny. Jewel only spoke to Sunny at the dining table. Roya felt that Sunny was a good name for her since her hazel-green eyes lit up the room, creamy complexion skin tone, and delicate features of an angel. Roya's other sister, laughing at the dining table, had to be mixed with Indian blood because of her dark reddish skin tone, and such a beautiful complexion, which any man desired to be with her after staring at her Coke bottle shape. Beyonce, look out girlfriend, you have competition! The other two sisters' names were mentioned through conversation among themselves. Sondrea seems to be the youngest of the pack. Her third sister, Lavonne, had a tan complexion and features that favored Roya, except her eyes, drooped downward. Her nose was longer with a slight pug and her lips were lusciously full. Roya assumed Lavonne was the middle child. Sunny appeared to be close in age to Roya. After glancing at all her sisters sitting at the dining table, eating, Roya jumped in the tub to clean the small wound.

Roya soaked in the hot water filled with bath bubbles and Epson salts. She felt so relaxed and calm. Then she heard her son crying in the bedroom, waking up from his sleep. She hopped out of the tub, wrapping a towel around her body, and walking out of the bathroom. She stepped into the bedroom and placed him in a car seat. She entered the kitchen as her baby's cries settled to a whimper. She sat at the table and glanced around. The voices of those around her became a buzz as she saw a hideous beast's eyes glowing red inside the dining room window.

The demonic creature's eyes stared at the ladies at the table. "Seeing who he can devour, conquer, and torture in the bottomless pit," she thought. Then, glass shattered. The ladies ducked and avoided the glass chips flying in the air. It reached through the window to grab one of her sisters. To Roya, the sudden stares of the beast reminded her of the beast in the "Tales from the Hood" movie. His claw-like nails hung out to pull his victim out of the house, but Roya offered herself.

Yelling to the creature, "What do you want?" She waved at the beast and then said, "Take me!"

Roya then shouted back to her mother to take care of her son.

The beast-like monster pulled Roya with his clammy, clawed hands through the window. It glanced back at her sisters, as they both flew like the speed of light.

She noticed, before he snatched her out of the home, the creature glared at one of her sisters to reach for, while two of them laughed endlessly. Their laughs still haunted her soul. She couldn't understand what could be so darn funny. If anything, this was a nervous, scary feeling that came over her as she glanced in his fiery-red eyes. Now she was flying in the darkness, seeing the moon glowing, as they soared miles away from her home. The stars glistened in the darkened skies.

"Now what? I won't see Mom, my beautiful son or my sisters ever again. Why did I open my big mouth and allow this creature to take me?" She was thrown into a bottomless pit. She watched others being tortured around her before her

humiliation begun. Some were tied to an electric chair, electricity shooting through their veins until their head blew off and repeated over, again. Then, suddenly, this same person was burning endlessly as the flames blistered his body. He prayed for water and for a way out. Women and men were naked, burning continuously. She knew her fate had come. She was being tortured with needles and knives stabbing into her skin. She could also feel the fire starting at her feet. And moving its way up. She didn't pray for water. She didn't pray for it to end exactly, she prayed to the one and only Lord. Jesus.

"Dear Lord, I'd like to confess my sins. Please forgive me if I did wrong to someone else. I gave my life to be sacrificed for the love of my sisters. I left behind my sisters and mother, and most of all, my only child. I left the love of my life. Lord, please forgive me. If I am meant to be here, please let me suffer." She bent her legs, and her body couldn't hold her up any longer as the flames became intense. It was smothering hot. Her lungs inhaled the smoke.

Her throat became parched as she gasped for air to speak, "I just want to praise you and continue to love you throughout this torture. Please, Lord; let me know if this is your will for me." Hot tears streamed down her face. She touched her cheek with one hand as it melted and glanced at her hand, watching her skin burn off. This was like a horror flick becoming a reality.

"I feel that I took my life for the souls of my sisters. I'm not sure which one was meant to be in this place," She cried.

However, she didn't burn to ash. Her body continued to resurface and re-burn.

"But I didn't want to see anyone go through what we're going through, here. How long will this take place?" She gasped as the hot flames filled her throat. She heard voices shrieking and screaming in agony.

She sucked in the smoke and tried to speak as her eyes burned from the smoky debris. "I'll continue to praise you like Daniel did when he was thrown in the Lion's Den. I'll continue to praise you like Joseph did when he was falsely accused and thrown in prison. This is worse than any prison. This is worse than being devoured by lions." She spoke rapidly, trying to release every word lingering in her spirit. She choked. Coughed.

"I feel the fire rising above my feet. Lord, at least, can I see Your presence." The fire exploded and burned her entire body, and repeated the process continually.

The creature howled and growled while Roya prayed. He heard all the others cry, whine, and pray for water, which made him laugh. Her prayer disturbed him.

"God will not hear you here," he growled. "He has commanded us to torment and torture those of the world for five months. Your prayers will not be answered. Give it up. You need to stop. You believe your prayer will end your torture!" He chuckled in a devilish laughter, and finished his statement saying, "Instead of trying to save your life, ask for God to end it for you," the hideous creature said. His horns resembled one on a bull, talons blanketed his body, and

sharp fangs hung as he spoke. His snake-like tongue she feared the most. Poisonous, she presumed.

'He wanted me to stop,' she thought. 'He wanted me to beg for my life. Beg for it to end. Beg for anything but to see Jesus!'

Roya continued to praise Jesus through the torture. She didn't understand what this torture was for, or its purpose. People were unable to get out of this dark, musky place, and will be tormented without any relief for a five-month period. Out of the blue, she saw a man come into sight in a white robe. "It has to be Jesus!" She felt His Holy presence. She heard a harmonious melody, as a harp and horns played a hymn of salvation. "Jesus answers your prayers." She watched as Jesus removed the fire from her feet, pain from her body and needles flew away. She looked around. We weren't in a building or warehouse. More like a cave, or inside of a mountain, or better yet, underground. Was this hell? I thought we die first? Jesus picked me up and ascended out of the place.

Her eyes opened, and Roya was back with her family. She shook from fright. Her body was chilled. She was soaked. She pondered on where this location could be? Her vision showed her Hell. When she awakened, Solomon gawked over her like a vulture over a dead body.

She started as she heard Solomon. "Baby, I thought I lost the love of my life. I didn't think you were going to make it." He took a moment before he could finish as tears rolled down his cheeks. "I prayed all night, and your mother did too. Jewel's still in the waiting room. I begged to stay here in this room with you until you woke up." He wiped his tears on his shirt sleeve. He sniffled harshly.

She heard the sincerity and compassion in his voice. Her eyes watered.

"You lost a lot of blood after you pushed the afterbirth. We thought everything was fine." He gulped. "The doctor demanded a blood transfusion. She was right." He shook his head frantically. "I thought the babies killed you." He paused with watery eyes. He reached for tissues to blow his nose.

"I'm so glad I made it." She said in a low voice. She then patiently waited to hear more, shakily.

"Not only that, you blacked out." The tears rolled down his cheeks. "I'm blessed that you're fine now." He looked up as if he was looking at the heavens and hearing angels singing praises. The relief on his face gave her hope.

He frantically spoke after his brief moment, "I heard you screaming with your eyes closed as if you were dreaming, a bad dream."

"I did?"

He nodded.

"So, I knew that you had to be alive and having one of your nightmares. I was here to hold you close to me." Solomon's uneasiness turned into gladness with the curve of a smile, and his eyes brightened as he kissed her on the forehead three times.

"I won't leave you," Roya said. "But my dream was so vivid that I thought I was dead and went to Hell, but I was tortured in such a place."

"What?"

"I dreamt this crazy dream. It felt so lifelike. I saw myself carried out of the house by a hideous creature. His wings flapped in the air, sounding like chariots of horse trampling in the wind. He took me to Hell."

"Hell?" Solomon quizzed.

"People were being tortured and burned without ever dying. Is that weird?" She shared her thought aloud.

He was speechless, only nodded.

"Maybe it was their souls continuously burning, but I could see their human form clearly."

She reached for his hand and cupped it into hers. "Solomon, I prayed. God saved me. Jesus Christ was present and stopped all the torture and burning that was ignited at my feet while moving its way up my body. Jesus removed me from this place back to my family."

"I'm glad that Jesus brought *you* back to me. Wait, did you say a creature?" He scratched his head. His eyes widened, "What did he look like?"

She shrugged.

"I believe that's in the Bible." He said earnestly.

Roya explained this hideous gargoyle-like beast. Most people would be terrified or laugh at such a dream, but Solomon took it to heart. He searched for a Bible. He prayed over the Bible for understanding and wisdom from the Heavenly Father aloud. Solomon flipped the pages until it stopped and kept the Bible open to the page he needed wisdom and clarification on the dream she had. The dream was indicating about the fifth trumpet sounded in Revelations 9. He read it to Roya.

"Then the fifth angel sounded: And I saw a star fallen from heaven to the earth. To him was given the key to the bottomless pit. And he opened the bottomless pit, and smoke arose out of the pit like the smoke of a great furnace. So the sun and the air were darkened because of the smoke of the pit. Then out of the smoke locusts came upon the earth. And to them was given power, as the scorpions of the earth have power." Solomon was interrupted by his wife.

"That's what I saw, Babe! The clouds were darkened, and so you're saying *this* creature came from a bottomless pit?" Roya batted her eyes in disbelief.

"That's what it seems, according to God's Word. Let's see where I ended." He put his finger on the spot. "And to them was given power—oh, I read that. They were commanded not to harm the grass of the earth or any green thing or any tree but only those men who don't have the seal of God on their foreheads. And they weren't given authority to kill them, but to torment them for five months. Their torment was like the torment of a scorpion when it strikes a man."

"Yes, I felt like needles or blades were sticking me with such pain!" yelped Roya as he tried to continue to read this chapter.

"My poor Roya. So you were tortured in the dream? But you admit that God rescued you out of this bottomless pit. It says, 'In those days, men will seek death and will not find it; they will desire to die, and death will flee from them.'"

"They did beg for death, water, or any way out of this pit," Roya agreed. Solomon still held the Bible open on his lap as he sat next to her bed.

"The shape of the locusts was like horses prepared for battle. On their heads were crowns of something like gold, and their faces were like the faces of men. They had hair like women's hair, and their teeth were like lion's teeth. And they had breastplates like breastplates of iron and the sound of their wings was like the sound of chariots with many horses running in battle. They had tails like scorpions, and there were stings in their tails. Their power was to hurt men five months. And they had a king over them, the angel of the bottomless pit, whose name in Hebrew is Abaddon, but in Greek, he has the name Apollyon. One woe is past. Behold, still two more woes are coming after these things."

"Whoa. That's what the creature looked like and sounded like."

"Really?" Solomon pondered.

"Yes. Wait, I also saw women in my dream that appeared to be my sisters." Her subconscious had revealed her sisters along with their names.

"Sisters? You never told me you had other siblings."

"It showed me in the dream," Roya explained. She changed the subject back to the creature and tortured for a period of time. "Is there a reason for him torturing people for *five* months?"

"It appears that they don't have God's seal in their foreheads."

"How will we know if we have the seal?" Roya inquired, as her eyes grew wider and mouth remained agape for answers.

"I'll have to research this more closely and look at the study Bible for a better explanation. I'll have to talk to the board about this!" Solomon exclaimed.

Curious, Roya asked, "What board? Your record label wouldn't be interested in this information, would they?"

"I meant this group of people that I'm involved in." He stuttered.

"What group? You're keeping secrets from me. You never did this before. Please let me know. Tell me." Roya folded her arms, sat upright to hear his answer and ignored the twitching pain after being stitched below.

"We can talk about this later. The nurse is at the door." Solomon's voice lowered.

The nurse entered the room to check Roya's vital signs and clean her up. "I'm glad to see you awake. I have to proceed with readings and cleaning."

"Oh, I thought that was already done. How long was I out?"

"I would say about thirty minutes. The doctor believes you were dehydrated, and exhaustion caused the blackout." She read the monitors and wrote it down on the chart.

"Oh." Roya sighed heavily.

Solomon stood by Roya's bed.

"Once you are done, can I see my babies?"

"Of course. One of the nurses will get a wheelchair and take you to see them." She then took her blood pressure, checked her temperature by putting the small thermometer in her mouth and beeped. She wrote the readings on the chart record.

"The doctor will speak to you in a while."

She exited the room.

Before Solomon was able to tell her more, the nurse came in with the chair, and wheeled her, with Solomon and Jewel following behind to the Neonatal Intensive Care Unit. Joyful smiles took over their faces as the three of them gazed at the newborns. Roya forgot what she and Solomon was discussing when she gazed at her caramel brown girl and boy infants. The nurse asked if she had names for them yet. She only grinned. She was thankful to have twins again. She named them, Solomon Jr. and Selena. Solomon was flabbergasted that Roya named the children after him.

After they heard instructions on helping their tiny babies feel loved and grow well, Roya, Solomon, and Jewel took turns reaching into the incubators and stroking the little ones.

She was overwhelmed and excited at the same time while in the presence of her children. Solomon kissed her on the lips.

"Roya, baby, you are the prettiest Mama on the face of this earth! I love you."

Roya glowed.

"I love you, too, Solomon," she said.

Chapter 13
Scandal Begins

JEWEL BATTLE

Florida
Jewel's attack while in court proceeding

Two months passed. The probation hearing date was at 8:30 a.m. Roya had Lisa Black, a neighbor, watch her children while she attended the hearing with her mother.

Jewel was a nervous wreck as they drove to the courthouse. Roya bristled at her mother's exclamations and the hand on her arm each time it looked like someone would cut them off in their lane.

"Mom, calm down. You seriously cannot be going inside the courtroom like that." Roya said as she parked the car.

"What! You are asking me to calm down, really? Give me some tissue girl. Do you have any in your glove compartment of this dang ole car?" Jewel's nerves were raging. Her face reddened, and she was perspiring profusely. She tapped her face repeatedly with a small handkerchief she found in her purse.

"Whatever, just let's go." She opened her door and closed it after stepping out.

"Alright," Jewel replied and, tapping her forehead, placed her handkerchief in her purse, she exited the car, slamming the door.

"Okay, mom! Geez. We have to trust everything is in God's will. How do you feel?"

"Ugh, it's obvious! Written all over my sweaty face," Jewel said sarcastically. She cracked a smile.

"Well, maybe it is best to keep my mouth quiet on this one," Roya smiled. She noticed, as they entered the courtroom, that Jewel didn't look so well. Her heart thumped with excitement.

The usual crowd of court observers entered the gallery and sat down. Inside of the courtroom, Roya watched as the judge proceeded to take her seat behind the bench. Then, she surveyed the courtroom to see her father's illegitimate children. Jewel, on the other hand, seemed to be more concerned about these other children taking her husband's pension check to accommodate these other baby mothers. She vocalized it numerous times before appearing in court that she needed proof: the paternity test. Jewel and Roya then heard the judge call the case.

"Battle versus Taylor, Willis, and Lathan."

Roya realized, when she glanced in Judge Collins' direction, that Jewel's annoying sighs and fake coughs were ignored. Judge Collins resumed with the detailed document before her, "The coroner or medical examiner also was able to retrieve Mr. Battle's medical records when he was last hospitalized before his death, and stored a blood sample noted as formaldehyde fixed tissue or paraffin block of tissue collected on his last hospital visit. They can test this to the samples on his DNA profile and then a buccal swab sample by each alleged person present here to verify the results for the child paternity tests."

When Judge Collins called the parties forward, Jewel sauntered to the front of the courtroom and stood in front of the judge's desk as Roya followed. Roya's eyes darted at those walking forward to the front of the courtroom. Jewel stood reserved but tapped Roya to stop looking their way.

She spoke quietly in Jewel's ear, "Mom, they look just like they did in my dream. Amazing."

Jewel lightly slapped Roya's hand while she shushed her.

The beautiful young ladies paraded alongside their mothers in the courtroom except for one. The first called to speak was "Taylor."

"I'm Mrs. Taylor, and this is my daughter, Lavonne."

"I'm Ms. Willis, the adopted mother of Sondrea since her parents were killed in an Iraq battle in the crossfire." She explained forthcoming with too much information.

"I'm Sunny Lathan, Your Honor. My adopted parents were killed last year in a car accident. Since I've come of age, I've been in a program called Independent Living. They are assisting me with my bills and an apartment that I just moved in a week ago, I only came here to, finally, see my birth mother," she shared without being asked by the judge.

"I'm glad to see that everyone is present. May we begin?" asked Judge Collins.

"Yes," responded Jewel. She anxiously tapped her feet and swayed her body.

"It appears that Mrs. Jewel Battle, widow of Lazarus Battle, requested genetic testing upon each person claiming to be a descendant of Sergeant Lazarus Battle. Due to the economic hardship this may create on Mrs. Battle's income, this request has been granted. Therefore, we honored this request and also to determine child support from his pension check, which is currently going to Mrs. Battle," replied Judge Collins as she shuffled the papers.

She steadily looked at the standing participants, all apparently eager to hear the paternity results. She sighed and spoke in a cordial manner to inform all parties of the DNA testing. "As some of you are unaware of DNA testing of the deceased, well, there are cases where the alleged father is deceased, and the Medical Examiner's Office or coroner needs a blood sample or tissue sample from the deceased individual. When the soldier was returned to the U.S., a blood stain card was collected from the deceased alleged father in this case. This is the ideal sample for a DNA paternity test."

"That's true, your honor. Please read the test results," exclaimed Jewel, crossing her fingers. Roya held her mother's hand down after that finger stunt as they waited to hear the outcome of the results of the paternity tests.

The judge cleared her throat, "Based on the Genetica DNA testing, a Family Reconstruction DNA test was performed. An additional test was done to test the genes of the deceased alleged father. She is present in our courtroom today, as a known biological family member. Those biological family members could be his parents, his siblings, or his known children."

Jewel's face registered anger as she blushed a reddish-pink in her cheeks when looking at her daughter, Roya. "You didn't!" She angrily exclaimed.

The judge pounded her gavel on the wooden platform, screaming, "Order in the court. Jewel, one more outburst, I will hold you in contempt of the court."

Roya remained silent on the retort coming from her mother. She did, discreetly, offer her DNA for the testing.

"According to the DNA tests, Lavonne Taylor is Lazarus Battle's child with 99.9% accuracy. Sunny Lathan is not Lazarus Battle's daughter after also testing his daughter, Roya Battle-Whitmore. Sondrea Willis is Lazarus Battle's child with 99.7% accuracy. It appears that, with the exception of Mrs. Lathan, these young ladies are Lazarus Battle's children.

"The court will allow his checks to be garnished to pay a third to each child he has fathered. You will still receive your pension, Mrs. Battle. None of these mothers are entitled to the amount that you're currently receiving. Once his payments end, you have responsibility for making these child support payments until they're eighteen years of age unless they attend college studies; in which case, you are responsible up to the age of twenty-five in the state of Florida." Judge Collins spoke without emotion.

"Hell, no, I'm not." Jewel cried out.

"Order."

"This woman, Lavonne, I believe, is her name—she has to be older than twenty-five years old. Therefore, she's not entitled to anything." She guessed. "My husband may have fathered these children, but no way in hell am I responsible for their child support payments since he wasn't married to them!" She fired back angrily. Face reddened; she waved her hands frantically like a mad woman. Roya stepped to the side to avoid getting swung on. Spit spurted from the corners of Jewel's mouth. Roya wiped her cheeks after getting sprayed by her mother's saliva.

Jewel shot more venom concerning the outcome, "Once his payments end, these payments of child support should end, too. From my understanding, these payments will not end since I'm his wife and married to him over twenty years."

"Jewel, I will have to request you to stop." Judge Collins exclaimed.

"I'm not responsible for these bastards! The government will have to make those payments!" screamed Jewel, eyes downward, not looking at any of them or the judge.

"What's wrong with her?" Mrs. Taylor nodded her head in disgust, looking at Lavonne.

Mrs. Taylor was suing for back child support for all the years she took care of Lazarus' daughter. Roya surmised, from Mrs. Taylor's expression, that she was just as surprised to hear that Lazarus had another daughter much younger than Lavonne and an older daughter married with children already.

Jewel continued. "Nothing, he shouldn't be paying for those illegitimate children!" She snapped her finger and pointed her forefinger in the air. She yelled angrily, "One thing I know now that they're my husband's, well I mean deceased husband's children, but now I have to allow the state to garnish his pension check! This is crazy! You got me twisted," She jerked her head and placed her hand on her hip with attitude.

Judge Collins tried to speak over the outburst but was not heard.

Jewel left the podium and walking towards the women on both sides, pointing in their faces before the Deputy left his post to hold her, "I'm just now getting on my feet, are there any amenities to stop this? I'm losing my darn mind!"

"Ma'am you have to go back to your post. Otherwise, I'll have to arrest you and throw you out of the courtroom for disorderly conduct." The deputy voiced.

Judge Collins hit her gavel on her desk. "Last time I will request order in this court. Order, order in the court!"

As soon as Jewel quieted, Judge Collins continued. "For the last time, Mrs. Battle, you will come to an understanding of proper decorum in this court, or I will have you jailed in contempt." She softened her voice, "I can only try to understand how you feel, Mrs. Battle, but this reaction will not proceed any longer in my courtroom."

Jewel tried to keep her composure and slightly nodded.

"It appears at this time that his checks will not end. However, do not anticipate that this will be a forever thing."

"Okay, what does this mean?" Mrs. Taylor inquired and her eyes nearly to a slit.

"The military has made payments for his funeral arrangements, and the pension goes to his wife. Once they calculate how long this shall be for the term he served, there's a high chance they will end."

"How will I know?" Jewel said with a twinge of anger in her voice.

"You can let the court know your status at that time, and we will handle their child support payments from that point. Again, I'm just informing you that there's a possibility these payments will be garnished from Lazarus Battle's pension check you're currently receiving according to the state of Florida. This concludes this verdict," remarked Judge Collins as she stood up and the gavel pounded down against the wood.

"All rise," spoken by the deputy as he walked back to his post.

Every person in the courtroom stood up from their seats as Judge Collins exited the room. Jewel was ready to leave until she was stopped by Sunny, who hugged her.

"I conducted research to find my real parents. You *are* my mother, right?" She spoke slowly in syllables.

"Yes," Jewel answered reluctantly. She kept tabs on the adoption process when she gave her daughter away at birth.

"Good. I'm so glad to find you." Sunny added.

Jewel grunted softly. "Uh-huh."

"Are you able to tell me who my father is since I didn't get the opportunity to know him personally?" Sunny asked.

"Prefer not to discuss here," Jewel spoke in a near whisper.

"I'm sorry to hear that your husband died in the Iraqi war, fighting for his country." Sunny sympathized.

✝ 135

"And how do you know this?" Jewel said sassily, raising her hand upward angrily.

"Newspapers. YouTube, of course." Sunny said.

"What do you want? Do you want more money? Do you want to live with us?" Jewel questioned Sunny and curved her lips sideways. She had a one-night stand, and her suitor was long forgotten.

"Dang, is it like that?" Sunny's voice rose. "I wanted to get to meet you in person and to get to know my family better. So, you're my sister?" Sunny turned and directed her question to Roya, ignoring Jewel's negative comment.

"Yes. I'm Roya Whitmore," she said, with a wide smile. She held out her hand to shake, and Sunny complied.

"Oh. I know you. You're married to that music producer and actor, Solomon Whitmore! Solomon Productions."

"I see you have done your research," Roya added, smiling.

"Hey, I can sing. Hopefully, I can sing for your husband and get a record deal. More importantly, I'm glad to meet you too," as Sunny reached her hands out to hug her.

Roya giggled, "Girl, do you know how many people tell me that they can *sing!*"

Jewel displayed her disgust with Roya being ecstatic to meet Sunny in person. She also had a splitting headache and toddled slowly through the exit doors of the courtroom. She titled her head to the side, rubbing her temples. Her husband's bastard children followed her, with their mothers creeping behind them.

"Excuse me, Mrs. Battle, I didn't deserve to be called a bastard," said Lavonne, and Sondrea nodded her head in agreement.

"Well, if the shoe fits wear it. Was your mother married to my husband, or even married at all?" Jewel retorted.

"Look, you don't know me, and apparently you didn't know your husband either. I didn't know the man was married, for your information," Mrs. Taylor said.

"Where did you meet him?" Jewel fired.

"I met him in Puerto Rico. He was stationed down there for a couple of months." She answered abruptly.

"I do not recall him stationed in Puerto Rico." Jewel blurted suspiciously.

"Secondly, I've been married to Mr. Taylor since Lavonne was two," explained Mrs. Taylor with her hands on her waist with an attitude to think she never was married.

"Oh." barked Jewel, trying to walk away. She mumbled, "I don't remember him stationed in no Puerto Rico. Not during the 'Operation in Iraq." She shook her head in disbelief.

"Look, missy." She took a pregnant pause. "I know that he loved me. We spent a couple of nights together and didn't expect to get pregnant."

"Really, loved you...uh huh."

"He treated me like I was the only woman on the face of the earth. How was I supposed to know that he was married?" Mrs. Taylor shrugged. "He even talked about marrying me for your info, Miss Prissy," She snapped, as she pointed her finger upward to get her point across.

Adrienna Turner

"Whoopie do. Apparently, you're not the only one he lied to." Jewel threw her hands up. "I assume he told Sondree, whatever your name is, told your mother the same lie!" Jewel fired back. Her words were hurtful because each face wore a pained expression. She rolled her neck and snapped her head back, turning away from them.

"Well, from what I have learned about my mother is, she was married too," Sondrea responded.

"So you are not sure? I take it that you researched as well," Jewel sassed.

"Before I was sent to my adoptive parent...I have my mother's locket that on my neck and her precious possession, her journal or diary. So my mother's from Afghanistan, not Iraq," Sondrea's eyes shot at Ms. Willis and then back at Jewel, "And my parents fled to America," Sondrea looked downward and tapped her foot while explaining what she knew.

"Wow," Roya gasped. She drew nearer to her youngest half-sister. "This must have been while the Afghanistan operation end of 2001 and then early 2002 the State of the Union addressed the operation moved to Iraq also known as the 'axis of evil'," She rambled aloud.

Sondrea continued her story in the court hallway as people strolled by. "Oh, really? This may explain why my parents fled to the U.S. However, I only remember a big fire, thinking our home blew up in smoke." She paused. All eyes were on her in disbelief or shock.

"While you were in Afghanistan during the war?" Roya inquired. "You must've been a small child."

✝ 138

"Yes. I was very young." She continued, "But the big fire happened once we moved to America. Your president speaks of terrorism, but I believe some radical people found out my parents were from Afghanistan and out of spite, set our home on fire. I vaguely remember how I lived but somehow was found on the streets."

"Really." Roya sounded skeptical.

"Some speculate I was carried on the angel's wings to safety. I was placed in a shelter ran by an adoption agency. I was only ten at the time of my loss."

"Sorry to hear that." Roya and Sunny chimed in.

"I honestly think and feel in my heart that my father wanted to kill her, and somehow the gas was escaping when he tried to light her on fire," Sondrea speculated, then continued, "Earlier, I heard them arguing. I only remember bits and pieces of the incident, but one of my earlier foster mothers researched further and told me before Ms. Willis adopted me," Sondrea stopped and looked around.

❀ROYA❀

Roya moved closer to Sondrea to soothe her, for support. *How brave she is,* Roya thought.

Ms. Willis covered her mouth with her hand in shock. "So you're not from Iraq?"

Sondrea shouted, "No." Then she directed her eyes and body turned to look at Jewel, "You have no clue about my conception and the hell I've been through..."

Jewel flagged them off and sneered, obviously not accepting these as her husband's children. "I'm sorry to hear that. But this is too much for me to deal with right now. I have a splitting headache, and I wish my daughter, Roya would come on."

Roya looked at her mother. Jewel's face was bright red, and her nose flared. Roya tacked what she observed to her mother's overreactions, and turned back to her sisters.

"I'm sorry to hear that too, Sondrea. I'm here if you need me since you're my sisters," Roya offered. "I mean half-sisters. This is a lot for me to deal with too."

"I am in shock too, to find out that the love of my life, in a short period of time, was married and fathered two other children besides my daughter, Lavonne." Mrs. Taylor shook her head. "I also saw on the news what soldiers' died for our country, and he was listed. I hate I couldn't attend the funeral." She digressed. "If you want to know more about my daughter or meet again, here's my contact information," Mrs. Taylor dug in her purse and passed out her business cards to Roya, Sunny, and Sondrea.

Seconds later, Jewel collapsed on the floor. Roya ran to hold Jewel in her arms as Sunny assisted and grabbed the other side of her body after falling to the floor. Mrs. Taylor called 911 and offered to stay and help. Roya nodded that it was okay and flagged them to leave. She'd already got her business cards before her mother's sudden fall. Sunny stayed with her as Roya waited for the ambulance to arrive. Roya reached for a pamphlet in her purse to fan her mother.

Several minutes later, the paramedics arrived, took Jewel's vital signs, and then carried Jewel to the ambulance on a stretcher. Roya asked to come along in the back of the ambulance truck, and so did Sunny. The paramedics politely explained they could not, but they could meet them at the emergency room.

Roya called Solomon, and he met her at the hospital.

Jewel's blood sugar was low. It was apparent that she was unaware that she was having diabetic symptoms. After Jewel had been stabilized, Roya was allowed to see her mother. Sunny followed behind as Roya entered the cubicle.

"You didn't have to stay," said Roya. She flagged her to go back out the hospital's exit.

"I wanted to, um, I mean be here, y'all know, by her side. Can I speak to you alone?" Sunny stuttered.

"Sure," Roya replied, seeing her mother was sleeping peacefully. She turned to go back to the waiting room.

She sauntered to a chair in the nearly empty waiting room. Sunny's head drooped as soon as she flopped on the polka dot couch near the chair. Tears followed.

"What's wrong?" asked Roya. She reached her arm over her shoulder and shook her next to her.

"Truthfully, I'm living out on the streets. I figured this child support would help me get my apartment back. They threw me out yesterday. I mean, I was evicted," Sunny sighed.

"So my mother was right, you're out for money!" Roya countered and removed her arm from around Sunny. The tension in the air was thick.

✝ 141

"No. I meant everything else I said. I was researching to find my birth parents. I'm not a charity case, just need a place to crash until I can pay the rent." Sunny elaborated.

"I can lend you the money." She exhaled in frustration. "Matter a fact; you don't have to pay me back!" Roya exclaimed, signaled to Sunny as a way to get rid of this pest of a so-called sister.

"Thank you. I appreciate it." She responded humbly and continued, "I'll talk to the manager today, and you can go with me to show that you will make the payment to stay there. I'm looking for a job now." Sunny wiped her tears and smiled. She sniffled.

"Wait, if you were evicted, not sure if they manager will accept you back in the apartment; but I can give you a good word if you need me," Roya changed her demeanor that flickered like night to day, and noticed her husband walking towards her.

Sunny nodded in agreement. Roya extended her arms to hug Solomon. He hugged her tightly with a tear in his eye. He planted a wet kiss her on the cheek. He was stunned by the resemblance in this lady, favoring his wife, especially Jewel. She sensed he noticed the resemblance to her sister, Sunny, after his eyes darted back and forth at Roya and Sunny.

"You must be Roya's sister?" He extended his hand to shake.

"Yes. You're Solomon Whitmore. Glad to meet you. If you're looking for a gospel singer, hit me up. I'm more hip-hop, contemporary, though," laughed Sunny, extending her hand out to shake his.

❈SOLOMON❈

Solomon responded with a sudden smirk. He turned to walk into the room where his mother-in-law rested on her gurney. He twitched his nose at that hospital smell.

He whispered to Roya, "Babe, what happened with the court dilemma? Is this what made your mom have this *fall-out* you called me about?"

Jewel shut her eyes as he drew nearer. Roya dragged him outside of the room to explain to him privately.

"Babe, she got flustered. I mean sweating profusely, shaky a bit, and then fell in the courtroom hallway when we were ready to leave. She got upset with the women who won the child support case of the girls that my dad fathered. It is a big mess!" She exhaled. "Luckily, Mrs. Taylor called 9-1-1 and Sunny wanted to follow with us."

"That is a mess."

"Can you believe not only did my Ma have an adulterous affair on my dad while he was deported to Puerto Rico, he supposedly met one of the ladies who conceived a daughter with him and other he met; in India, I think. No Iraq. Wait, it was Afghanistan."

"Okay, which one?" He joked.

She threw her hands upward. "To add to that, this woman cheated on her husband and died in some explosion once she came to America."

"Who did?"

She continued, "Maybe, he found out Sondrea wasn't his daughter." Roya rushed through the details which Solomon gave her a quizzical look.

"Who's Sondrea?" Solomon asked when he heard the name come up in her discussion about the court hearing.

"She's my half-sister by an Afghanistan woman, and the other is Lavonne Taylor who's from Puerto Rico."

She sped through the info. "I think the whole ordeal really got to mom—she went ballistic!"

"I can see that," He chuckled then composed himself after seeing the angry expression cast over Roya's face.

"Like the doctor said, at least now we know she's a diabetic, and thankfully she didn't have a stroke...um...but her emotional status, she went ballistic on something seeming to her unrealistic...then fainted outside of the courtroom," Roya sighed and exhaled heavily.

"Whoosh, Babe, let's go back inside and check on your mom," Solomon advised. He lowered and nodded his head in hopes to calm her.

He opened the door and blew a kiss to reassure her that everything will be okay when she glanced at him. Jewel smiled when she saw them.

Chapter 14
What's Next?

SOLOMON WHITMORE

Florida
God's Tabernacle Church

Isaiah orchestrated a private meeting at God's Tabernacle Church promptly at 7:00 p.m. He instructed Solomon and several males to teach constructional gatherings held at God's Tabernacle Church.

"Welcome new and seasoned leaders. I would first like to start this meeting by introducing you to Solomon Whitmore." Solomon stood up from his seat as members cheered and clapped while he walked to the podium. He lightly bowed.

Isaiah appointed and anointed Solomon Whitmore as the associate pastor. The others eyed Solomon attentively. Solomon shook nervously. Isaiah handed the microphone to Solomon to say a few words.

"Thank you all for coming out for this special event. As you know, Isaiah had televised sermons to gear others to the same mission God has for us in this time. Yahweh has exposed the unseen world, mysteries, and gave Isaiah revelations to share with us in these last days." He coughed. He swallowed saliva and cleared his throat to finish his statement, "God promises in His word that man will dream dreams..." He paused as he glared at the men's faces. He saw anxiety, fear, and even doubt in the few faces he saw before cautiously continuing.

"I read last night in the book of Numbers chapter 12 that the Lord came down in a pillar of a cloud, stood at the entrance of the tent when he summoned Aaron and Miriam, saying to the two of them, 'Listen to my words: "When there is a prophet among you, I, the Lord, reveal myself to them in visions, I speak to them in dreams."' Yahweh, the Lord that came to Moses, called I AM that I AM, spoke to Moses...just like He is speaking to Isaiah. With no further ado, I will allow the man of God, the prophet in these end times, speak the message he received directly from the Lord." Solomon carefully handed the microphone to Isaiah. He wiped his sweaty palms against his pant legs.

"Thank you, Solomon. Bless you also, man of God." He patted him lightly on his shoulder before Solomon positioned himself to take a seat. "In this *unseen world,* we are facing a spiritual warfare, battling against angelic and demonic forces, right here in the earthly realm." He pointed downward. "We can find these answers in the Book of Daniel. I charge you to study the Word for yourself." He pointed and eyed each man. "We are the walking examples of Christ, he overcame for our benefit, and we will soon be experiencing the Great Tribulation. Let's put our talents, abilities, and skills into action." He animatedly demanded. He waved at Solomon to return to the podium to speak to the congregation.

Solomon extended one hand for the microphone and shook Isaiah's hand with the other. The words spewed hurriedly from his lips with depth, "Well, well, well." He raised both hands forward and clapped lightly. "We are glad to have you all here, especially our new brothers in Christ Jesus." He then rested his hands on his waist near his midsection. "I know some of us don't like to, um, be called the "Bride" of Christ," Solomon said jokingly.

Chuckles and coughs filled the room.

"Well. Let me first start by saying that I met Isaiah almost a year ago at a church sermon on a teaching called "Revelation." This particular sermon wasn't only shocking, but startling, and scared the living boo-boo out of me." He paused while the laughter blared in the room.

"So after all that, we made a spiritual connection and this man, Izzy, is my spiritual brother and leader. Those of you who don't know him, I want to tell you his credentials." He read his notes, "He holds graduate degrees in Pastoral Counseling, Psychology, and Theology from Valley Forge, Southern Illinois, and Marquette University. He is a licensed psychologist and ordained minister. I am so honored to serve with and under this man." He slightly bowed, and eyes darted at Isaiah as the other men in the room eyes followed suit. "I just want to add, we are blessed to know and have all of you here to serve too." He lowered his head to a nod. His eyes shot at another member and pointed to indicate he should take the mic.

"Thanks, Solomon. I want to say to those of you who don't know this brother," He side hugged Solomon as he went on, "Get to know him. He has a sincere love for others and especially God. God has a purpose for him and meaning for his life, gearing and teaching men to fear the Lord as well as being ready for the Apocalypse. He flagged another male to come to the podium. "Well, here's my other brother in Christ, he joined Alliance Crusaders for Christ too. Please welcome Joshua Mack." Isaiah said cheerfully and waited for the applause to die down.

❋JOSHUA MACK❋

Joshua stood upright, lightly shaking his dusty brown wavy hair, and held the microphone tightly once handed to him. "Yes, I am the fair skin brother with hazel-green eyes— also called yo 'brother' from another mother!" He said jokingly. He heard the chuckles in the crowd.

"I want to make y'all feel like y'all belong. Look, I came from a dysfunctional, broken home. Well, I guess all of us come from some dysfunctional family. But both of my parents were on drugs, linked to prostitution and horrid life on the streets. Um...I know race doesn't matter here once we are bruthas in Christ." His dialect was slang and sounding East Coast.

Joshua continued, "My mama was part Hispanic, from Spain, and Caucasian, I believe, and pops was Italian, what a combo, mafia, pimp, and big-time hustler. His half Hispanic and Italian father was a pimp and big time hustler. My ma was his high-scale prostitute." He paused and coughed. Isaiah waved giving an indication to continue when Joshua glanced at him.

Isaiah reached for the other microphone. "Joshua suffered from gossip, slander, and rumors and has been laughed at and talked about on the streets as well as school grounds. He fought to prove his manhood, what he stood for, and his peers about the rumors said about his parents. He was later awarded to the state and disowned by other relatives because of his parents' not so good lifestyle. He's also been molested by foster parents, older siblings, foster relatives, and been abused all kinds of ways imaginable." He took a moment to gather his thoughts.

"He was dramatized and drawn into a lifestyle of drugs and alcohol. He drowned his problems in liquor, ecstasy drug, marijuana (weed), and whatever he could get his hands on." Isaiah added.

Joshua nodded to finish. "Well, I finally met Isaiah. Or should I say that God united this connection? He found me on the street corner, down and out, bumming for change." He lowered his head as if he was about to cry. "Even my old lady back then kicked me out of her house because of stealing, cheating, and never getting a job. But this man, right here, my homeboy Izzy took me." He patted his chest as it thumped loudly. "He trusted me in his home...a stranger y'all. You know that scripture where Jesus talks about; did you feed me, clothe me, etc.? Well, this brother did this for me." He pointed directly at Isaiah in the audience. "He even hooked me up with a job. He made me go talk to someone, get counseling; and I saw some psychologist for free. I went to rehab too." He smiled with glossy eyes.

Joshua added, "But Isaiah spoke about the goodness of his Heavenly Father and how much He loves him. How He has a purpose for all of us." He raised his hands and extended them. "He also displayed love by taking *me* in his home with his family. I felt like the prodigal son coming home to his father." His head lifted as a lone tear rolled down his cheek. "I was clean from drugs and alcohol about a good year now."

Men stood up and clapped.

"I received a degree in computer technology," he said, as the applause grew louder. He heard a few cheers.

"The one that Izzy recommended me to back then and now volunteer as a Youth Minister and help with the youth as Assistant Pastor. I'm a man who doesn't like titles but for those of you who want to put two-and-two together...now you know." He pointed his two fingers together. He then crossed his first two fingers to demonstrate how close Isaiah and he were now.

A few amen's blurted in the audience.

"I know there are other brothers here, who want to testify and tell you why we are united as brothers in Christ...but Isaiah didn't only help me get on my feet, but to find the Lord." He made a fist and shook in an up and down motion. "This man is a great example of who we are to follow, Jesus! He let me know he cares about me, loves me, and shared the gospel." Joshua explained with glee.

Isaiah said, "Thanks, Joshua. It was my pleasure to help you and see the man God knew you would be. He has more coming.'Y'all, as he would say, ain't seen nothing yet,'" he paused as applause erupted. "We are also working on his lingo or dialect too. But more importantly, Joshua gave his testimony to the youth to get them on fire for the Lord. He reached many, who gave their lives to Christ, and found their purpose under God's will too." He smiled and clapped while people joined in for Joshua's testimony of hard times turned around.

Other members joined the organization that night and testimonies continued as each verified their faith in Christ.

❋ISAIAH E WILLIAMS❋

Isaiah delivered his message to his congregants. He turned to the book of Daniel to emphasize the power of prayer. "My brothers, I'm glad that you're here tonight. We're bringing more brothers to these meetings, amen to that and a couple shared what God placed on their hearts. Men, we are the head and not the tail. We are the *head* in our families to carry the vision and message from Christ. Turn with me to the book of Daniel." He put on his reading glasses.

He paused to let others open their Bibles or use their tablets to get there. His voice lowered for a moment while explaining, "While I was looking at the book of Daniel, Daniel didn't accept the new law by King Darius in Daniel 6:8-9 and Esther 8:8. In Babylon, what was the king's word was the "law," and King Darius allowed pride to take over. Once he had a little power, he passed a law to be worshipped and praised for thirty days by the people in the land."

His voice escalated an octave, "For a whole month, there will be men and women who will worship and praise this man also known as the Antichrist. A man I say." He cleared his throat and eyes shot at each person in the room. "Did you hear me?"

He heard a few yeses.

He finished with a forceful gesture, "To worship and give praise to a man, is that outlandish?" He stared at the group of men and saw the mixed expressions. His voice changed to a calming tone, "However, Daniel stood alone. He was a man of God and didn't pray to the king. But, Daniel prayed three times a day to God. He had a disciplined prayer life." He slowly pulled his reading glasses from behind his ears. He rested them quietly on his Bible. "Don't you want to get to that point with the Lord? We can. Prayer is just another way to talk to our Heavenly Father." He sounded reassuring.

"For example, Joshua was a man who followed Moses. He trusted God and once that leadership was passed on to him, no doubt, he was afraid of such honor. He didn't think he could step forward with this task to lead the Israelites once Moses died."

"Tell us more, pastor." A man in the audience shouted.

"Imagine that, a man who fought armies to make it to the Promised Land!"

"Fought to get to the Promised Land." Someone shouted in agreement.

"However, he had a prayer life and honored in God's eyes and later took the baton of leadership over the Israelites into the Promised Land. He did whatever it took to glorify the Lord and follow His will." He paused to take a sip of his bottle water and glanced at the strong, faithful men in the congregation. He hoped they got the message of what to come in this age.

"Back to Daniel, *prayer* is a lifeline to God. It continued throughout our lives, not just when we need something or in trouble or going through the motions, but even to praise the Lord through the good times! Praise Him." He clapped as the others shouted, "Amen" and "Hallelujahs" as he choked for a moment and took a couple of gulps of the water before continuing. He wiped his forehead with a handkerchief.

He licked his lips and spoke with authority and power, "Daniel didn't hide his daily prayers to the Lord during this trying time. Conspirators caught him even in secrecy to make sure everyone was following this decree. Don't you think hiding would've demonstrated that he was afraid of other government officials, and as Christians, we're to fear only the Lord."

He said with authority. "Daniel continued to pray, he couldn't look to the King for guidance and strength during this difficult time; only God could provide what he needed most. Once it was notified to the King, there was a punishment that followed for not honoring his law. We have to face consequences for our actions even with God. It may not seem like it at the time, but eventually, we'll pay the cost for our sins." He saw the fear in some men eyes.

He said confidently, "I know that Jesus Christ died on the cross to pay the debt of our sin—the wages of death.

However, it's like a child who disobeys its parents; a normal parent would place them on some type of punishment, restriction, or old school parents would spank their children for being disobedient. Well, God will spank us for what we've done as well." He swayed his hand as if he was spanking the air. He emphasized the word *spanking* to get prepared for the demise that lies ahead. The creases formulated on his forehead, as his breathing labored. He could see the expressions of the men, and clearly denoted they were getting the message delivered.

"So the punishment was to be thrown in the Lion's Den. Can you imagine yourself in a Den full of hungry, furious lions ready to devour and eat every ounce of flesh from your bones?"

A few no's spurred in the room.

"However, in Daniel 6, verse 16 states that God shut the lion's mouth so that unbelievers were able to witness the power of God and Daniel's consistency. You may be asking, what consistency? Consistently is relying on God for answers, for guidance, for recognition, for praise. Do we turn to God?" His voice cracked and then fanned himself and wiped his face with his white handkerchief.

He carried on with the sermon for the male members in attendance, "Are we ready, friends? That's why God called me to have this meeting, to create this organization Alliance of Crusaders for Christ." He lowered his head for a brief moment. "One day, that time will come, it will be a reality. No longer are a dream of disaster, but a reality and we're living in a hell. This is more or less to deceive us to believe in world peace. This world peace is another form of power, pride, and evil forces of Satan. This is why we're preparing like Joseph did in Genesis 40 or 41, after interpreting Pharaoh's dream, precautions were taken." His voice became raspy.

He took another swig of water before finishing his viewpoint on what is taking place today versus that in Daniel's timetable.

"We're taking those precautions as I mentioned in an earlier meeting. For those that were not here, when the Antichrist rises, he'll find a way for people to make a choice. We'll either to receive his supremacy and take the mark to symbolize this choice or to be killed."

"Killed?" a male voice said.

"If not, we'll be killed for the simple fact that you'll not accept the mark and for most of us, a follower of Jesus Christ. However, if we don't accept this mark of the beast, human number 666, which in a dream, I see as a drawing of a flower." He stops talking to show his diagram on the projector screen.

"I will not take the MARK!" another male stood and shouted.

"This flower isn't an ordinary flower; it's made from these 666's. But, since early 2000, Verichip is a company that supplies microchips will be implanted is apparent to a technological symbol of the mark." He showed the illustration on the screen and then shows another screen with both images vertically, side-by-side.

"When will this take place?" a male asked.

"Soon!" Solomon responded.

"Therefore, we're planning ahead, since we have signs that it's near."

"Yes, we are," Solomon added with a pounded fist in the air.

"From each president or world leader, we see signs in democracy, in the law, with people and things in the world. Bible speaks of it loud and clear." He pounded his fist on the transparent stand.

Isaiah paused, and eyes scanned the room for Solomon and pointed his finger at him in the room, "But, the precautions we are taking are saving food, clothes, and other ways of survival in warehouses."

"This is true, Pastor," Solomon exclaimed.

"We're learning self-sufficient skills as they did in the Old Testament when they didn't have technology, electricity, cars, and all the materialistic things of today." Isaiah finished his preparation speech.

Some of the heads followed Isaiah's forefinger pointing at Solomon who humbly bobbed his head as Isaiah finished his sermon and message to all the followers of Jesus Christ.

"Yet, I think we'll need technology skills since they'll implant these chips in our hands or foreheads."

"We're ready." Joshua nodded.

"More importantly, we're to trust in the Lord and obey His will. God, delivered Daniel, will he deliver you? Will you allow Him to speak to your heart? Do you trust the Lord's will with all your heart, mind, body, and soul?" Isaiah repeated the last two statements as the members echoed it, loudly, in the sanctuary.

"Daniel had a vision of great beasts, 'World Empire,' which is what we are preparing for. God let me know that it's near." His eyes darted at the congregant that inquired during his sermon. "It's similar to King Nebuchadnezzar's dream in Daniel 2. No matter what happens, God will conquer them all."

Isaiah continued as his voice deepened, "This will happen to us sure enough once this Antichrist reigns. He'll kill anyone that doesn't receive the mark and especially Christians or anyone that follows Jesus Christ. More than thousands of Christians have been killed since 1999 in Nigeria, and nearly 1,000 homes and churches have been burned down by such radicals-all because of their faith in Jesus Christ. Stand up Brother Malik." Isaiah waved his hands upward for Yosef to stand up.

Yosef rose from his seat as Isaiah had commanded. "See our African friend, Yosef Malik, has been a great help with this organization as a student from West Africa, Nigeria, as I'm sharing in this sermon. We hear thousands are still being sacrificed for their lives for believing and serving a Mighty Yahweh. His faith is beyond what any man here can ever experience because of his witnessing deaths like I described here."

Yosef agreed with a nod. He sat down a moment later as Isaiah glared back at his notes.

"Therefore, we created ACC, Alliance of Crusader for Christ, to provide help for those who will not receive the mark. We're preparing before this time comes."

"Amen."

"Also, we're blessed to have carpenters, computer technicians, web designers, and practical workers to create and come up with vehicles that operate on solar energy. We've stored food, fluids, and clothes for family members who will not receive the mark; and other solutions to hibernate once this occurs to keep a distance from Antichrist and his followers." He took a sip of his water. He carefully observed each man in the building. He then picked up his bottle of water to gulp a few sips down.

"These are signs that the time is near. We'll talk more in depth on this topic. Please take your manuals home to research and study the Word as we'll talk about it more openly next time. Next week, we'll discuss these great beasts. We'll also allow open discussion for strategies and to get ready. The Bible speaks about watch and pray. Let us pray." Isaiah knew he spoke much longer than he anticipated.

He had to close with prayer. "Dear Heavenly Father, thank you for sending your Holy Spirit with us today to deliver your message to your people. Lord, continue to show us your will for our lives, and we are here to do as you ask of us. Please grant us travel mercies on our way home and as we leave this place. In the Lord's name we pray, Amen."

❀SOLOMON❀

Members bade one another good-bye until their next meeting. Solomon moseyed to the back of the building and noticed his wife standing with hands resting on her waist and eyebrows furrowed with a smirk on her face. Obviously, Roya knows where he's been. He knew she presumed he was MIA: missing in action, especially when he says he's at the studio. Solomon shooed her to leave the premises, but her mouth opened and the words that flowed from her mouth couldn't be unnoticed by others passing by.

"What are you doing here?" Roya said nastily.

He shrugged. Silence was golden.

"I wish you would've told me! I drove all the way to the studio looking for you! Burning all this gas in the tank and this time I decided to follow you!" She exclaimed.

Her voice rose, and she snapped her finger with a twirl, "No. A matter of a fact, I detected your phone using the GPS app!"

"Wow." Solomon shook his head.

"Why could you not tell me the truth of your whereabouts? I would've understood," Roya lashed out as Solomon drew closer with his arms extended for a hug. She flicked his hands away from her.

"Did you hear me?" She rested her hands on her hips.

Solomon did not respond to her verbal lashes. Her mood and tone of voice shifted from angry and agitated to soft spoken and calm, "I've overheard a bit of the sermons shared when I slipped in. So we'll have to store food, clothes, etc. to get away from the *Antichrist*?"

Solomon lightly nodded and rubbed his goatee.

"I know that we talked about this in church, but come on seriously? You expect me to believe this? This is too much to take in at once. Whoa." She sighed heavily.

"Regardless of your secrecy, I'd like to help in any way I can." She licked her lips. "Why are there only *men* in this congregation?" She glanced at most of the men exiting the building while waiting for a response.

There was an awkward silence. Before Solomon calmed her ill-temper, pulling her outside of the building to discuss it further, Isaiah drew closer to them. It was obvious he couldn't ignore her comments and wanted to answer them personally. Isaiah stepped away from the door and walked outside to have a word with her.

"You have a good question about why there are *only* males in our meetings. First, we have to find strong men who can lead. We've also thought of including women soon. I'm glad that you spoke of it, though." Isaiah raked his goatee.

"I would like to see you at our next meeting and any other females that wouldn't be skeptical of this concept." Isaiah proffered.

"Ok," Her voice lowered to a whisper.

"I received this from the Heavenly Father. In addition, we can use more people to prepare for this dreadful time that is set to come."

"Yes, we do." Roya folded her arms.

"We're seeing signs all over the world; however, at this time we're still free to worship. We should take advantage of this opportunity." He introduced himself. "Hello, let me properly introduce myself, I'm Isaiah E. Williams. Solomon is our second in command leader for our organization. I'm glad to meet you," Isaiah shook her hand.

"I'm Solomon Whitmore's wife, Roya, and glad to meet you as well." She said hastily.

She took a double look. "Wait, I saw you on television awhile back, some private network paid by Isaiah E. Williams. Yes!" Her eyes lit up.

"But you mentioned that you need strong men. It takes devoted women, wives, and sisters to make these strong men you speak of. Men come from the womb of a woman. Remember that." She snapped her finger with force.

Isaiah's face beamed, followed with a smiled, and shook her hand before he could respond, Solomon yanked on his wife's arm.

"Now, can we go Roya? You're welcome to come to our meetings at 7:00 until 8:00 p.m. I'll explain the rest to you this evening once the kids are sleeping and your mother is out of our hair. We've been waiting on her hand and foot since she left the hospital," Solomon said, holding her hand and walking her to the parking lot.

Roya made no comment.

Chapter 15
The Meetings

ROYA WHITMORE

Florida
Saved Disciples Association

As Roya began participating in the meetings, more women were involved, and then the youth. The youth were to carry the baton of hope to the world. Things were changing rapidly, and no one knew where to turn, except to Jesus. There were so many false teachings and religions. She taught a class in the women's Bible study. She shared imperative information from a book, *Unleashing the Spirits,* written by Adrienna Turner.

"I want you to think with your spiritual mind before making any decisions." She raised her forefinger to the temple of her head.

"This simply means speak to God first. For His Spirit resides in you once you become a believer in Jesus Christ. Open your minds. Open your hearts." She said passionately.

"We have to be ready for persecution. We are challenged with the government forcing us to take the mark. Some call the device RFID, meaning radio frequency ID for identification. Tracking. Others call it the microchip." She pressed to the next slide of her presentation. She glanced at the expressions on the faces of the congregants.

"We cannot submit to the ways of the world. We cannot make excuses for taking the chip to eat, buy or sell. Can you believe they wanted me to sign a document after having my twins to insert the chip in their precious bodies?"

Some hummed in astonishment.

"So we have to prepare for destruction for the believers. But the church is going to do Christ's work throughout the world. This means us. We are the 'church'." She paused. She gulped saliva.

"For example, Paul knew that the Thessalonians would face pressure from persecutions, false teachers, worldliness, and apathy to waver from the truth and leave the faith. Therefore, he urged them to "stand fast" and hold on to the truth. We also may face persecution, false teachings, worldliness, and apathy. We should hold on to the truth of Christ's teachings because our lives depend on it. Never forget the reality of Christ's life and love!" She inhaled and slowly exhaled.

"Look to God for wisdom. God gives wisdom freely to all who ask." She lightly nodded.

"When we see evil leaders who live long and good leaders who die young, we may wonder if God controls world events." She shook her head lightly.

"In the NIV Study Bible tells us that Daniel saw evil rulers with seemingly limitless power. Daniel knew, though, and proclaimed that God 'removes kings and raises up kings'; he controls everything that happens." She studied the facial expressions of her class before continuing and reviewing her notes.

She gasped for a second, and her chest heaved as she continued, "Some Christians fear that any mistakes we make in our normal lives will destroy their witness for the Lord. They see their own weaknesses. If an individual stumble, the rest of the group is there to pick him or her up and help him or her walk with God again. If an individual sins, he or she can find restoration through the church, even as the rest of the body continues to witness God's truth. As a part of Christ's body, do you reflect part of Christ's character and carry out your special role in His work?" She left the congregants with the question to meditate on and silenced herself.

Solomon and other volunteers ministered to the youth group. After several months of leadership at the Alliance for Crusaders of Christ (ACC), Isaiah no longer delivered sermons at his previous church. His main focus was in these informational meetings and formulated it into a congregation of lesson planning and preparation for imminent catastrophes including seismic changes predicted to happen.

Chapter 16

Lost in a Fantasy or Reality?

ROYA WHITMORE

Eight months later

Roya expressed her delight to have Solomon home by bringing him breakfast in bed, wearing lingerie, and performing short, tempting dances for only his eyes to see and a body to enjoy. He blocked touring on his schedule, but still sampling and mastering recordings in the recording studio.

He also participated in ACC meetings. She missed being with Solomon while he was on the road. Before they had children, she would travel with Solomon, and loved being inside the trailers for his movie roles or taking music artists on the road. She would call him on his cell phone, and he'd give her his hotel and airline flight information to meet him. More than anything, Roya missed holding him and making love at the spur of the moment. She also missed wearing sexy lingerie inside of a trench coat, ready for any and everything. And then, she missed kissing his luscious lips, hearing his sexy voice talk sexy-nothings in her ear, and how she could feel his heart beating when he held her near.

She also thought about showing up at the concert and seeing his Chester the cat smile cast on his face. She desired him strongly now after letting these memories bounce in her head. But, she thought, every time they do get their groove on, another conception in her fertile womb.

The Bible speaks about loving God with all my heart, mind, soul, and body. God is the one that blessed me with this union of marriage. I have to defuse these negative thoughts! She rested on her knees praying for the family and her husband. "Lord, I hope he's fine. I know that temptation is out there and presented in front of him all the time." She gasped as she visualized Solomon present. "Solomon isn't only sexy, but a cutie and loaded with money from his acting career and music production as a business man. God, keep him covered with your shield of protection and covering from these lustful devils." She ranted.

Roya tried to call Solomon's cell phone number again, pressed the TALK button again to redial his number automatically. Finally, she heard the phone click over as if he picked it up.

"Hel-lo." He moaned.

"Hi, baby. Is that you? You sound like you've been sleeping. Did I wake you?" asked Roya.

"Yes. Is this my sweetie-poo? Roya is that you?" He whispered and voice cracked.

"Yes. I miss you so much. I need you."

"I'm almost done mixing this..." Solomon whispered. "Wait...I fell asleep in the middle of the mix."

"I miss how we use to kick it. How I use to appear at your shows, etc.?" cried Roya.

"I hear you, baby. I feel the same way. I was just lying in my bed, imagining that you were here like old times." He hummed with an exhausted moan. "I thought that you'd secretly hide in the hotel room and come out in some revealing, sexy lingerie."

She recalled that memory and made a low moan.

"Darn, I miss you. I wish you were here, right now." His voice sounded sexy on the other end. He paused.

"I'll be home, as soon as possible. I love you." Solomon convinced Roya.

"I love you too. Let's imagine we're together right now." Roya replied. She rested firmly against the fluffy pillow and closed her eyes as she fantasized.

"Baby, I'm not sure if this is a good idea. Phone sex?" Solomon's voice escalated to a high pitch on the other end, and then his tone, deepened as he said the words *phone sex*.

"Calm down baby. I want to do it. You don't have to get turned on then," Roya replied with her body temperature rising.

"What do you mean? I'm a man. I'm human. I have hormones too." He rambled. "Once I start imagining you here with me, I can easily get aroused. I know that we're married, but a man can only take so much from his wife."

"Whaaaat." She whined.

"Right now, I'm asking you not to talk or try to turn me on at this time. I got to do this video on the set tomorrow early. It's exactly at sunrise." He carefully explained. "I need to go back to sleep. I have to get up in a couple of hours." Solomon yawned.

"Fine, Solomon. So much about this marriage and you're not meeting my needs! Bye!" as Roya slammed the phone down on the cradle. *Ooh,* oozed from her lips. She grew highly upset and wanted to satisfy her hunger by talking dirty and self-pleasing herself.

As she entered the bathroom, the phone rang. She ran to answer it after washing her hands. It was Solomon.

"Hello."

"Hello," Roya repeated. "What's up, Solomon? I thought you didn't want to talk to me?" asked Roya, sitting down on the bed and pulled the covers up.

"Baby, are you alone?"

"Yea. Why?" Roya inquired. He didn't sound groggy or sleepy like he did an hour ago.

"I'm coming to get you," Solomon said, in a creepy voice.

"This isn't *Night of the Dead* or one of those horror flicks with that creepy voice you're making. What's up?" Roya inquired with sass.

"Are you still mad at me?" Solomon asked, waiting for her to reply.

"I was. Will you quit playing with me?" Roya questioned and sounded agitated.

"Open the door. Are you in the bedroom?" Solomon replied.

"Yes. Why?" Roya quizzed, as lines formed on her forehead.

"What are you wearing?" He asked inquisitively.

"The usual." She responded dryly.

"Is it that little thing I like?" Solomon queried.

"And you know this." She emphasized. "Why are you playing on the phone? Now you're in the mood? You're down to have phone sex?" Roya fantasized, asking Solomon what he thought.

She flopped down on the bed and anxiously waited for his next response.

"I got something better. Surprise," Solomon screamed *surprise* as he opened the bedroom door with his arms open wide. She didn't hear him tip-toe up the stairs.

Roya's bottom lip dropped, and she fell back against the headboard. She rubbed the back of her head and jumped out of the bed to run into his open arms. She kissed his cheek to his nose and then his forehead.

She squeezed Solomon until he tapped her on the shoulder, "I can't breathe, Babe."

She loosened the embrace, and he pushed her backward onto the mattress. He climbed on top of her and kissed her neck, lips, and slipped his tongue inside her mouth. French kiss. Roya stopped before Solomon took off her robe and lingerie.

"Shh. I think I hear the kids," She brushed him off of her.

"I'll be right back. Let me go check on them. Lie down and keep the bed warm until I return." Her words escaped from her lips in a seductive tone.

She quickly tiptoed into the infants' room and rocked them back to sleep. After taking about thirty minutes to settle the children down, she sashayed in the room and found Solomon sound asleep. *Dang!* She missed out on some action and pure satisfaction. She sneaked out of the room, after seeing him sleep peacefully. She wanted so badly to disturb his rest, but she knew that he was up all night and day working on that video for his musical artist, and took a flight to come home as he had promised. He could've waited until the next day to come home.

She longed to make love to her man. She stepped back into the room. She crawled on top of him and kissed his moist puckered lips. Then she kissed his forehead, licked his eyebrows and down to the middle part of his nose; back to his lips. She unbuttoned his shirt, and kissed his chest. Solomon awakened from his sleep to find his wife on top of him, kissing and sucking on his upper body. Roya made it clear to Solomon how she desired him. He allowed her to proceed, enjoying every moment of it. His wife was the boss and took full control over the situation.

After they had enjoyed their pleasure, they heard their elder children waking up, hyperactive and ready to eat. Roya quickly went to shower away the musky smell of lovemaking. Solomon came into the bathroom, and pulled the shower curtain aside, to see her nakedness. He grinned. Then, he climbed into the shower with her.

She responded to him, "No," since she knew that it would lead to more lovemaking.

Solomon fooled her. Roya guessed he heard the toddlers' cries too. Instead, Solomon washed her body and lathered the soap with his hands onto her back; the water streamed down her flesh. She took a hold of the soap and did the same to his body until they were squeaky clean.

Roya reached for her nightgown robe on the bathroom door, raced down the stairs to the kitchen. She grabbed the egg carton out of the refrigerator, cheese, turkey bacon, bread, hash brown patties, and pancake mix with bananas. Then, she mixed the pancake mix with crushed bananas; put the bacon in the microwave to cook, and hash browns in the oven. She made toast for the kids. Her eyes beamed when Solomon stepped in the kitchen to eat breakfast. More than anything, she was flabbergasted that Solomon was home with his family. She wished the kids were in school, and just the babies were home.

❖SOLOMON❖

Solomon. I've been thinking..." Roya said subtly.

"About?"

"Our youngest twins will be one soon."

"Are you serious! I don't think I can do this anymore." Solomon contested.

"What are you saying," Roya folded her arms after she nudged him with her fist.

"Time is going by so fast." He quickly added.

"Sure is." She cut her eyes. "But things are changing rapidly. I think the government will interfere again to get the babies chipped. They want our children chipped next school year, and I strongly refuse this notion."

Solomon sipped on his coffee with a slight nod.

"One minute they're born, and now they're toddlers," smiled Roya as she was feeding them in their highchairs. She eased back in her motherly duties.

"Man, the times are moving quickly," he commented. His train of thought changed the subject, "Baby, I'll be done after this video shoot, and you'll be busy again. I saw that you were offered a role an upcoming movie. What is it called again?"

"*Beauty to Ashes*. Cloud Ten Pictures are the one doing the project. I had to be on a strict diet and six-day workout to get this figure back. Come to think of it; I haven't been in a movie since we did that one together. That was before we had kids." Her eyes looked upward, and she tapped her temple with her forefinger.

"I think it was before we were officially married too. For the movie: *Mystic Realms*. I couldn't believe that I was playing the main role as Vashti, and you were that no-good-boyfriend, Jordan. That was the same day that I fell deeply in love with you on the movie set."

"I remember."

"Poor girl in that movie according to the novel, I can see how easily she was deeply in love with a man who lost his life because of a freaky one-night love affair with a mystery woman and lost his happiness to be with Vashti and their child. Later he discovered the child wasn't his anyways."

"Yep."

"I love that movie. I watched it the other day. Maybe that's why my mind was totally on you and wanted you so much, and then you appear. A dream comes true!" Roya explained.

"Sure does."

Tavon and Javon walked past and made goo-goo eyed faces.

"Yea. I know. I was feeling you as well. We played that role so well; I couldn't believe the feelings we had off the set. They always had to say, "Stop. Cut." We would still be kissing whenever we were together. We were bad back then." He chuckled at the thought.

"Yea. When we got married, we were worse, look at *all* these kids!" said Roya as she washed the dishes after they finished eating.

"Not all my fault. What can I say? Come to the love doctor and let me take all your pain away and replace it with pleasure!" He said, in a Dracula-like, seductive tone.

"Stop or else I'll have to take you up on that offer, Mr. Solomon Whitmore. Watch your mouth in front of these kids," replied Roya as he came up behind her and hugged her from behind.

The doorbell rang. Tavon and Javon ran to the door, asking "Who is it?" Solomon followed behind them as they opened the door. He was surprised to see his parents at the door. He gave his father a smirk and lopsided smile.

"Hey, Son. What's the look for? Are you tempting my authority? Let me get my belt," said Solomon's father jokingly as he unloosened his belt from the buckle on his black dress pants.

"Dad. Quit playing. How are you, Mom?" as Solomon strolled over to hug her. Then, Solomon's father let a lash from the belt go on his bottom.

"Dad, stop." Laughter filled the room even Roya stepped in and laughed.

"Hi, Mom and Dad." She hugged them both and continued, "I'm glad to see you. What brings you guys here?"

"You guys aren't happy to see us?" Mrs. Whitmore said, jokingly.

"Of course, but it's a pleasant surprise. Normally, you two plan your trips and contact us first to make sure we're home."

"We're making plans to go to Disney World at the spur of the moment, right, Solomon?" Mr. Whitmore said abruptly.

"Yes. We were talking about going to Disney World. So what brings you two here, though?"

Solomon tugged on his father's shirt and gave him a look; *you shouldn't have said anything.*

"I wanted to see the kids. I miss them, and they're getting so big. Also, we haven't gotten the chance to see the new set of twins." Mr. Whitmore questioned.

"Would you like to hold them?" asked Roya, handing over little Solomon. Selena snuggled in her Daddy's arms. *Hmmph!* Roya thought. *Why do they come to see their grandbabies now? My mom's been around since they were born.* Mrs. Whitmore sat in the living room, pulling out gifts and handed them to the kids, one by one.

"I love you, Solomon. If words could only express how you make me feel—when you walk in the room and how my heart pounds when you leave. I'm so happy to be your wife. Don't ever leave me," Roya ran to Solomon to plant a kiss him on his cheek. Solomon hugged her and lifted her in his arms.

Mrs. Whitmore smiled, "I'll just leave you two to yourselves. I'll check on the children."

Solomon watched as Roya kissed him, his neck, his cheeks, and his lips again. She couldn't stop kissing his lips, his cheeks, all over his face.

"Are we still going to the amusement park?" Solomon threw his hands up.

"Sure. Are you ready now?" Roya asked in a childish voice.

"Yeah," Solomon answered back.

"Can I have an appetizer first?" Roya replied, saucily.

"What are you talking about?" Solomon was clueless.

"You can find out. Watch and feel," as Roya lowered her head.

Solomon displayed his eagerness after seeing his wife's sudden actions. Roya wiped her mouth as they walked out of the room. The kids were excited and ready to go to the amusement park. Solomon invited his parents to go along.

"No, this was for you kids to be alone with your family. We'll be here when you get back," Mr. Whitmore said.

Chapter 17

Disney Fiasco

ROYA WHITMORE

Disney World

The Disney World trip didn't go as planned. Solomon became exhausted after talking to his wife, and she ignored his plea. He exclaimed that he was ready to leave the amusement park.

"Come on boys, let's go. Exit the park to the parking lot. Help me load Selena and Junior in the Escalade."

Roya's lips were shut tight and silent on the ride home. As soon as Roya greeted Solomon's parents once they returned home, she entered the bedroom to pack her clothes, underwear, and cosmetics. She decided to get the kids in the morning. Joy flopped on her bed and shut her eyes. Javon and Tavon sauntered to their rooms and shut the door. They were drained and physically tired after so much excitement and fun at Disney World, with a long drive back home.

Solomon's parents left with smiles across their faces that night. She figured Mrs. Whitmore got her groove back on with Mr. Whitmore in their home. She studied Solomon's facial expressions, reading him clearly that he desired her to stay home and not to make a fuss in front of his parents before their departure.

She exited minutes after they departed. She drove to Jewel's Florida colonial home, where Sunny resided, after taking care of Jewel's business affairs once she returned to California. Sunny opened the door after the doorbell rang. Her eyes lit up, and mouth widened to see Roya standing, in tears, outside the front door.

"Hey, where are the kids?"

"I needed a breather. I had to get out of that house." Roya sounded frustrated.

"Okay. But after whatever this is," she waved her hands in a circular motion in front of Roya's face, finished her statement, "you better go get your kids!"

"Yeah, ok. Move and let me in." Roya brushed past.

Sunny said in a jovial manner, "You know you are too *pretty* for petty. You're too cute to be mute. Don't pout let it out?"

"Girl, stop playing!" Roya cracked a smile and followed by a light chuckle.

"Come on sis, what is it this time? What Bro do?" Sunny folded her arms as they walked to the living room.

"Okay." She huffed and titled her head back slowly. She lowered it and glared in her sister's hazel eyes.

"You sure you're ready to hear this?" Roya said hesitantly.

Sunny waved her hands to come on with it. She sat on the couch as Roya stood up.

"Well, I saw this chick on my man's jock. She acted like his wife wasn't even there, girl!"

"Really."

"She was all over him, touching and pursing her lips as if she was going to kiss him. When I approached her, and the kids were there too, she blew me off."

"So what'cha do?"

"So you know I snapped, and the rest is history! We left and didn't talk to each other on the ride home." She raged.

"Whoa! So you didn't get up in that butt?" Sunny joked.

"This trick didn't know how to act. I was about to whoop that to teach her a thing or to, but Solomon made me walk away, saying," She deepened her voice to imitate his, "'It isn't worth the confrontation...you're my wife and she's not. Didn't you see I didn't even pay her no mind? So get your mind out of the gutter and be a mother!'"

"That doesn't sound like Solomon but dang girl. That could've been on a reality show!" Sunny joked and giggled.

"Not," Roya yelled.

"Roya, you're blessed with a multitalented man. You'll let all of this go over something petty," Sunny said.

Roya didn't answer.

Then Roya wondered where her mother was. "Sunny, where's Mom?"

"Oh, mom. Girl, mom's dating a wealthy entertainer from BET. I think she's back in California. She hardly calls. She's dating a younger man too. I believe he's around our age group." Sunny pointed at her and her sister expressing the age factor.

"You're serious. Mom, come on. How did she meet him?" Roya intuitively asked.

"She ran into him at a restaurant I think." She tapped her temple. "Or a gas station pumping gas." She snapped her finger. "Well, he was attracted to her and spoke to her first. They exchanged contact information and went from there." Sunny spoke with uncertainty but answered respectively.

"I'm so happy for Mom. Man, I'll have to discuss this further when she comes home. I'm ready for details!" Roya exclaimed. She was enthusiastic and flabbergasted at the same time about Jewel's companionship.

Roya wondered if her father's behavior had an effect on her marriage and relationship with Solomon. She shared her concern with her sister. "Mom's heart has been broken so many times. I'm amazed that she was able to raise me like she did."

"Look, Roya," Sunny answered, "you can't always be about Mom. You got your own family, and it hurts kids not to have their family." She coughed. Her eyes became glossy. "Come to speak about family...you need to go get yours!"

Roya shook her head in frustration.

"Look, sis, I oughta know what life is without family. I looked for Mom for years." A lone tear ran down her cheek. "Maybe you should talk to someone about it, instead of making it about Solomon's weakness."

Roya considered what Sunny said. *My kids are important. Why am I not more worried about my behavior around them than Solomon's? Do I really need help from a psychiatrist? Sunny's right, at least let me get my kids and bring them back here.*

Adrienna Turner

Then, Roya felt the Holy Spirit fill her soul, whispering in her ear. 'Roya. You need to drop your self-pity party such as the accusations against your husband. You're to love your other half as the Bible commands. 'Wives, submit yourselves to your own husbands as you do to the Lord. For the husband is the head of the wife as Christ is the head of the church, his body, of which he is the Savior. Now as the church submits to Christ, so also wives should submit to their husbands in everything. Husbands, love your wives, just as Christ loved the church and gave himself up for her to make her holy, cleansing her by the washing with water through the word, and to present her to himself as a radiant church, without stain or wrinkle or any other blemish, but holy and blameless. In this same way, husbands ought to love their wives as their own bodies. He who loves his wife loves himself. After all, no one ever hated their own body, but they feed and care for their body, just as Christ does the church—for we are members of his body. "For this reason, a man will leave his father and mother and be united to his wife, and the two will become one flesh." This is a profound mystery—but I am talking about Christ and the church. However, each one of you also must love his wife as he loves himself, and the wife must respect her husband.

'Roya you are one flesh with your husband. Nonetheless, Solomon's your husband and has brought to your attention to get into the Word, and you'll find Me. I love you, my child. You have a gift. Express and expose that gift through your writing; Terry will give you this opportunity in his stage production. Learn and seek the kingdom first. I'll always be with you, my child. I love you Roya. Take up the cross and follow Me.'

While the Holy Spirit spoke to her, tears ran down her cheeks as she wiped her eyes with the back of her hands and then searched in her purse for the small tissue packet.

Voice-activated command picked up on her iPhone, showing Solomon's cell phone number.

Solomon picked up, "Hello. Roya."

"Solomon, I'm so sorry. Will you please forgive me? I love you so much and didn't mean what I said...I read the Bible and God has spoken to my spirit about how to set aside my desires and to refocus on His desires for my life. It is God's will, not my own."

Solomon listened and remained silent.

Chapter 18
One Step Further from a Blessing

SOLOMON WHITMORE

Florida
Jewel Battle's Mansion

Solomon drove to Jewel's home to bring more luggage in response to the call he received earlier from Roya.

"So what really brings you here, Sol?" Roya sassed and placed her hands on her waist.

"Um. You called, remember?"

She slightly nodded and folded her arms.

"You needed me to pack the kids' school clothes." Solomon offered without her asking. He changed the topic, "You have no idea how much I need and love you. I miss you." Solomon voice lowered and sounded sincere.

"Humph. You don't know—" Roya was cut off.

"Hey, Dad." His sons said in unison. He group hugged his sons.

"I see you brought our stuff, and our video games!" Javon yelled with excitement and shook one of his video games in his hand.

"Oh, you really want to play that...you know I will win, right?" Tavon teased.

"Boys. You see your father and I are trying to talk." Roya spoke harshly.

"Alright, mom. Chill." Javon eased back slowly with his hands in the air.

"Dad. What is really going on with you and mom?" Tavon inquired.

"You would have to ask your mother," Solomon said abruptly.

"Oh, why don't you ask your father about him going on another business trip. And something about his project manager..."

"Roya. Please. How could you let this be?" Solomon drew closer and attempted to embrace her, but she took a few steps back.

"Sons. I received a call from my production manager," His eyes shot at Roya, correcting her. "I will be cast in an upcoming movie with a small role but a great opportunity." Solomon waved at his sons to come closer.

"Dad, we got it," Tavon answered before his father could say another word.

Javon nodded in agreement. "Bye Dad. Get me a souvenir."

Solomon smiled.

"Where's my princess?" Solomon wondered.

"She's sleeping. She watched a Disney movie and fell asleep early." Roya offered.

Solomon kissed Roya on the cheek. He whispered, "Good-bye. I do love you."

✝ 183

Adrienna Turner

He pivoted back towards the door, "Roya, did you hear me? I love you."

She folded her arms against her chest. Her glare was deadly.

"I'm not really sure why you're so mad at me. Whatever it is, I hope when I come back that we can discuss it and work it out."

"Uh huh." She tapped her foot. Tavon and Javon raced to the door as their father exit.

"I'll try to call you when I get the time." Solomon glanced at Roya and then shot a gaze at his sons.

"Boys, be good to your mother and give my love to my sweetheart and my dearest Joy," Solomon said as he marched to the limousine waiting near the curb.

"Bye Dad." They said in unison. "We'll talk to mom."

They said and stared at each other finishing each other's sentence. Tavon socked him in the left arm. Javon chased him to the room.

"Tavon. Javon. Go to your room." Roya shouted.

"We are Mom!" Javon yelled at a distance.

✼ROYA✼

Late that night, Roya was watching BET music videos with Sunny. Roya stood in front of the TV, blabbing about something irrelevant, as Sunny interrupted her.

"Roya. Turn around. See who's on the television screen!"

"Who?" as Roya turned and stood near the end of the loveseat.

She stood speechless. Roya and Sunny watched a video featuring Solomon and Golden Brooks as the starred characters. Star 6 performed their latest hit song, but Roya's eyes were focused primarily on a relationship between the two. Golden Books kissed Solomon passionately—so convincing. His tongue hung low, touched the tip of his chin, as Golden Brooks hopped on his lap in the diner scene. The couple in the video was no longer eating their meal ordered; instead Golden was licking on Solomon's tongue.

Roya placed her hands on her hips and pouted. She cussed her insecurities loudly. She bit her tongue as her family watched the video too.

Tavon said, "Mom. Dad looks great in this video."

Javon added, "Really? Nah, Golden looks fine with a Y."

Sunny giggled at Roya's obscenities under her breath and her sons' outbursts. She then pressed REWIND on the DVR to view the video several times.

"Correction bruh. It's playback. I want to see Golden again and again and again." Javon jerked his head and then stuck out his tongue.

Roya slapped his forehead. "Boy, keep your tongue in your mouth."

"Down boy." Tavon joked. He hopped back and put his hands in midair. "Okay mom, just playing with my young bruh."

Sunny added, "This is what they do for sex appeal and to sell the song." She kissed her fingertip and swirled it in a circular motion to indicate how hot she thought the video was.

"Oh whee, Auntie," Tavon said eyes darted from Sunny to his mother then brother. He sat back in his seat, placing his fists against his cheeks, glued to the television screen.

Sunny sung the words to the song, "I want to get with you, girl. The passion drives inside. Feelings I cannot hide. I felt you were my story. The woman I was searching for. You bring me glory. Once you walked through the door. Kisses galore. Girl, imagine what I got in store. I can only imagine you in my arms. Heavenly skies. Can't deny. How I feel for you. How I love you. How I want to be with you always."

Roya squirmed, wishing Sunny would stop singing that song. She even covered her ears with her hands.

At the end of the video, the couple jumped in the latest Benz with the drop-top down as the wind blows her wavy weave in the air and he glances at the model while driving and singing the chorus, "How I feel for you...How I love you...How I want to be with you always."

Roya inhaled, exhaled several times with her hands crossed against her bosom and kept switching legs as she crossed them. She looked like she was going to *bust the move.* Lastly, she dissected the meaning of the video. Further along the video, she noticed that Solomon and Golden where at the mansion home in the backyard near a pool, as Golden sashayed in a revealing skin bikini, hardly showing anything for the imagination. She scanned at the house closely in the video and hit PAUSE.

"Heck nah. Solomon's doing this video at the beach house! The crew restructured the scenery near the backyard with a black-steeled gate around the pool and cement instead of sand with a Jacuzzi installed nearby the swimming pool by the patio sliding doors." *That bastard*, Roya thought in her mind. She paced back and forth, groaning loudly. She then said aloud and gritted her teeth, "I wish he'd called me before doing this video!"

"Mom come on. Seriously." Tavon raised his hands.

"Are you kidding me?" Sunny added.

"Yeah, Mom," Javon said laughing. "You know you loooove dad...just a video, not reality."

"Boys, it's your bedtime." She yelled and pointed in the direction to their bedroom.

"Really mom." Tavon pouted.

"Go now. Don't make me say it twice." She forcefully pointed.

The boys slumped out of the room.

"Come on Sis. Check with his wife before making this video, not going to happen." Sunny said, shaking her head.

The remaining part of the video showed Golden Brooks on his lap, kissing and entwined together as a couple in love with a smile on their faces. Roya wondered why they didn't show the group hardly in the video. Then, she read the credits to see that he directed the video. Solomon couldn't blame someone else for this music video since he was responsible for the direction of the video as the executive producer and director. *How could he?* Her thoughts fluttered, *Was I losing my touch? Was I gaining weight? Was I less attractive to him? Or could I just not be all that I'm supposed to be as his wife!*

❀SUNNY❀

Sunny stared at the stress lines on Roya's forehead with her nose flared as tears streamed down her cheeks.

"I understand that it's just a video, but come on," Roya stressed.

Sunny attempted to hug her.

"Does he have to do all that kissing? His tongue stuck out and letting her lick it for the world to see? Come on, bruh. That's too much to sell this group's music." Sunny admitted casually.

"Sunny. If that was your husband, would you feel the same way about it? It's just a video." Roya rambled and pondered on the question.

"Yes. You're taking things out of proportion just a tad bit. You need to learn to trust and love your husband. He's a music producer, creative soul, music video producer, and director, as well as actor." Sunny offered.

"But we are Christians and have to set the example," Roya interjected.

"Believe me, when I say this, you're lucky to have him. I mean truly blessed. You need to stop tripping."

"Sunny. I'm tripping," She said, batting her eyes.

"Geez, what has come over you these past few days! You need to let it go." She snapped her finger in front of her face. "Let God work it out. I can understand some of your anger, but it's useless. You're making a fool of yourself," said Sunny. She stood at attention and pointed at parts of the video on the TV that weren't worth getting angry about.

Roya exhaled noisily and lifted her right hand as she nearly slapped the smack off of Sunny for her insensitivity until Selena crawled in the living room. She picked Selena off the wooden floor and placed her back in the bed until she fell asleep. Sunny glanced at the clock and pressed the remote OFF, and then crept into her bedroom, crawling into bed without the blankets. Roya stormed inside Sunny's room and gawked at her.

"I can't wait to see *you* get married someday, if ever. Then, we'll see if you feel so liberal and okay with the fact that the world is looking at her husband making out with a woman on the video screen," Roya whispered and puckered her bottom lip.

❊ROYA❊

She walked back into the living room.

Suddenly, she heard keys jingling. The door flew open. Sondrea.

"What are you doing here?" Roya said aloud.

"I live here. Mom didn't tell you?" Sondrea barked.

"You're serious. Mom? She allowed you to live here." Her eyebrows rose slightly. "Of course, she didn't tell me; otherwise, I wouldn't be in shock to see you here."

"Okay." Sondrea turned her head in the other direction.

"How old are you again? You may look older, but if I'm not mistaken, you're only like, sixteen?" Roya wondered what she was doing out and coming in so late.

"Um, time has passed since we last saw each other in the courtroom." She answered hastily.

Roya's eyes narrowed. "Wow. Yep, you're so right. Excuse me. But what are you doing out so late or, should I say, 'early' in the morning?" Roya speculated.

"Look, Roya. You don't know me and my situation," Sondrea sassed and shook her forefinger directly at Roya. Her voice escalated, "You don't live here, so this is none of your business."

Sondrea walked past without looking at Roya's squinted eyes, and voice cracked, she said, "I'm tired and hitting the bed. Peace. I'm out."

It was obvious to Roya that their discussion was putting Sondrea in an ambivalent disposition.

Roya fired back after she entered her sleeping quarters, "No she didn't talk to me like that. I'm her elder sister, no matter what she thinks. I'll have to set her straight in the morning."

Then, Roya's mobile phone buzzed. She saw the virtual reality images of Solomon's face displayed on the phone screen. His facial expression broadcasted sadness, loneliness, and emptiness.

"I missed you. I want to be home with you," Solomon cried with a twinge of bitterness.

"I miss you too. I cannot accept this type of lifestyle anymore. I'm losing it, baby." Roya couldn't believe she said that to him. "I don't know why I keep snapping about women coming on to you. I should've known when I married you what I'd deal with. I know you can't control other people's actions, such as touching you. I want to ask you something," Roya sighed deeply.

"Anything," Solomon replied.

"What's up with this video with Star 6? The video is *How I Feel about You*." Roya was curious about his direction on the new video Solomon directed and produced.

"Yes. What do you want to know?" Solomon said naively.

"You know exactly what I mean...!" Roya voice rose and deepened as she angrily replied.

"Dang. We have to go through this time and time again. Don't we?"

"Okay, Solomon."

"Puhleese. Can you come home? I can explain it to you then." Solomon pleaded. "Yes, I know your next question is. 'But didn't you direct it?' Yes, I did. I took the leap to do what they were singing about in their latest debut track. I couldn't get an actor to portray the role; so since no one would get it right, so I did it." He said.

Roya was quiet.

"Roya. Roya, I know you can hear me."

Silence.

"Are you there?" He questioned.

Dead air.

"Babe, it's just a video!" Solomon said pragmatically and carefully watched his words.

Roya knew that he didn't want to upset her even more, but she couldn't bite her tongue any longer.

"Stop there. It's more than just a video. You minister to the youth, remember? You talk about the music, songs, raps, and videos they watch today. What are you portraying in this video? Imagine if they saw this?" Roya waited for an answer.

"Oh, it's like that. I get it. Was it the kissing part that perturbed you the most?" Solomon teased.

"Yes. Do you know how humiliating it is to see you kissing on a gorgeous woman in a video like that? How many people saw that video and wondered too! It was so sensual and sexy. I'm not sure how much I can take with this career." She ranted.

"I see your point." Solomon agreed.

Roya sensed he did not want to fuse her anger and continue to argue over the phone.

"Maybe I should go back into making movies or star in someone's video, and then we'll see how easy you'll respond when I kiss another man so sensually."

"You're taking it too far."

"You know what? I'll stop tripping since Sunny asked me to." She slurred and overly emphasized the word *tripping.*

She added, "Maybe I need to get out of this house and cool off. They're sleeping, except the boys are studying for their mid-term exams."

"Not leaving our kids with your sis Sunny are you?"

"You are not okay with that?" Roya puckered, but he heard the sass.

"Not sure it is a good idea."

"I promise, they'll be fine. I love you too. But, I had to speak my piece," Roya said as she blew a kiss on the phone.

"I'll be there shortly! Love you more. Thank you." Solomon's voice sounded overjoyed. He puckered his lips to make a kissing sound *muah* and pressed the END button.

❋SOLOMON❋

When he returned home from his business trip around 4:15 a.m., Solomon rushed to Jewel's house and picked up Roya and the kids. He helped carry the sleepy toddlers in the car, securely strapped in the car seats, and then held sleepy Joy in his arms and propped her in the car, strapped her in as the boys drooped in their seats. He drove home while Roya's eyes became heavy. She dozed off until he parked the truck in the garage. He wouldn't allow her to touch a finger as he carried the toddlers in the house and held Joy's hand as she waddled inside the house, still sleepy. The older twins were wide awake and stepped in the house, giving their parents a weird look, but seemed glad they resolved their marital problems.

"Dad. What is going on with you and mom?" Tavon asked and broadened his shoulders.

"I hope we resolved our disagreements. Nothing to worry about *us,* Son." He patted his shoulder. "Best for you to go to bed."

"Sure, dad," Javon eyes widened with curiosity.

✝ 193

Solomon gave a nod. "Divorce is not an option."

"Before we go to bed...there's something we need to tell you," Tavon said, changing the subject.

"Okay, Son." He stood and folded his arms.

"Well, our school is requesting us to get these chips in our hands," Tavon said. Javon shook his head.

"Chips! How are they requesting such a thing without asking your *parents*?" Solomon's voice escalated.

"Mom got the letter in the mail. Notice. First, they are making the suggestion. Then, I believe it will be mandatory in another year."

"What? She hasn't told me," Solomon exclaimed.

"They have already introduced this to schools in California, Illinois, New York, and most of the Northern, Southern, and Western states. They started with the mid-west states but now it is going to be in Florida." Tavon explained.

Javon added, "Yeah, Dad, and then it'll be national."

"They say it'll make testing easier, and they're going to know which kids need remedial help. And they'll keep track of the younger ones, so people can't hurt them."

"Boys," Solomon sighed, "There is always a downside. Where is the letter? I want to read this." Solomon eyes darted at his sons and then glanced around the home.

"Dad it's late. We can discuss this further in the morning. I will also find the letter to show you. I think you have to sign it anyways. It requires parent's consent." Javon spoke before his brother could say it.

"This sounds like something that cannot wait. I am surprised I did not hear this from your mother."

"Dad, she went to the kitchen. Talk to her," Javon waved. Tavon followed suit.

Solomon entered in the kitchen. His face changed. Roya got a glass of water and sat down. Solomon sensed she was silently thinking in a dark room. It seemed a bit odd, but he knew his baby was sulking, yet desired him at the same time to tell him to get her at that hour. He came closer to her without touching the light switch.

"We need to talk. I know it is quite early, but the boys told me about chips being inserted in the kids, required in their schools now."

"I forgot to tell you."

"Roya, this is important and how could you forget such a thing!" Solomon said angrily. "Where is the letter or notification?" He slapped his palm into his hand.

"Somewhere." Roya shooed.

"You are still focused on that video! Are they also requesting this from our daughter, Joy?"

Roya nodded.

"We seriously need to talk about this with Isaiah and the others."

"Why? They are not the government..."

"So are you going to allow this?"

"No. They tried to insert those chips when the babies were born, remember? Selena and Solomon Junior." She explained. "We did not give our consent. I see what you are thinking...I will not give my consent for this either. We can deny the action at this time. You forgot I used to practice law. We still have rights."

"Soon those rights will be removed." Solomon's voice grew stronger and deeper. "Case law can change or be amended."

"Are you suggesting Martial law?" Roya asked.

He nodded his head. "Where the military gets involved."

"I hear you. But as you said, it is early, and the kids are asleep or headed to bed. We need to do the same." Roya suggested.

Something told him that she let those video images continually play in her head. She had this look to kill. He noticed a dim light near her. She had watched the video on her smartphone. He reached for her phone on the counter. He pressed PLAY. In the video clip, Golden fingers moved gracefully across the piano. "Humph." He slammed the phone against the granite counter.

"What is wrong with you? Trying to break my phone!" Roya shrieked.

"I want to chat about the microchip, and you're worried about this video. We need to focus on heavenly things, remember?" Solomon exited the kitchen. Roya followed him to the bedroom. She reached for his arm and then clasped his hand. He spun around. She stepped on her tip toes and gave him a wet one. His face softened. He kissed her back passionately.

"We can talk about it in the bedroom."

"That's my girl," Solomon smiled.

Chapter 19

Blessings in Disguise Hung in the Midst

ROYA WHITMORE

Florida

"Roya. You know that I only call you when I need your help. You helped me a while ago and so grateful for you and your husband to take care of me after that fainting spell at the courtroom. I think it was too much to handle..." Jewel sounded distraught.

"Okay mom, what do you need?" Roya asked.

"I heard you already saw Sondrea here. She told me about your episode," Jewel opened.

"Ugh. No telling what that girl said. Anyways, yes, we had our spat. Let's get beyond that. What do you need? Spit it out, mom." Roya said, sassily.

"Well, I need help with her. She needs to cool off. She has been dealing with a lot since I got her. She's going through the motions. You know how teenagers are." Jewel said casually.

"Nope. Not yet, anyway. I was only a teen once. I don't recall you calling grandma about me." Roya said.

"Okay. Well, I want the best for Sondrea and think she'll do better if she stays with you for a while until we get this matter situated."

"What matter, Mom?"

"Well, Sondrea is acting out. She's out 'til all hours, refusing to obey the rules of our house. She's drinking, probably drugs, and she's promiscuous."

"And I need to do what? She's not going to grow up until she's on her own for a while. There are places for kids like her."

"Maybe if she knew what it was like to deal with younger kids."

"Mom it just sounds like she is more than you can handle. You know I already have five kids in our home. Will she help me out too?" Roya snapped.

"Sure. Just ask her," Jewel said. "Well...can you do it?"

"Yeah. I'll talk to Solomon, and I'm sure we'll help but the minute she causes chaos and hell in my home, she goes back to you!" Roya stressed.

"Okay, got it loud and clear. Bye."

Chapter 20
Wildin' Out

ROYA WHITMORE

Los Angeles, CA
Whitmore Mansion

Roya and Solomon agreed and allowed Sondrea to move in the Los Angeles home with them while they worked on their contractual projects for clients. The Mansion home was spacious enough to house each of the children, with extra rooms for guests.

Solomon had a get-together party with friends and business partners. His business party promoted his musical artists while various music companies were present and agents. He faced negative connotations in the media, heated controversy about the sensual video he did with Golden Books. Even the congregation, Alliance Crusaders for Christ, questioned Solomon on the video. He made an announcement that he was no longer directing music videos and planned to proceed with acting opportunities.

Celebrities, actress and actors, and music producers including A&R people enjoyed the festivities inside their mansion home in Los Angeles. Solomon agreed to sign Sunny to Solomon Productions, Inc.

Roya spotted Sondrea drinking, wobbling and flirting loudly with male celebrities to be in their movie productions. Roya was glad she asked Jewel to look after the younger kids before the event began and drove them earlier to Beverly Hills. Roya's eyes bulged when she saw Terry Perry at the event. Terry maneuvered through the crowd to approach her.

She extended her hand to greet him, "Hello. How are you?"

Terry shook her hand and replied, "Fine. Thank you for asking."

"I love your plays. I thought Mr. Brown was hilarious, especially the funeral scene," Roya continued to select and discuss specific scenes his past movie productions for a few minutes. His eyes beamed and bobbed his head in agreement at her comments.

After their brief conversation, Terry offered Roya a part in an upcoming movie adapted from one of his plays. He asked her also, to direct the casting call for other actors and actresses. Minutes later, after Terry walked off, Mr. Johnson also approached Roya with a movie offer. Johnson's suave voice charmed her, and he asked her to be the screenwriter for his upcoming project, requesting the publishing rights to her novel, *3 Strikes to Disaster* for a movie. God had answered Roya's prayers. This was an outlet for her career to surface on the main screen again. She missed acting and the limelight. She only premiered in one major movie production as the main character and as extras or supporting character in several previous movies. She was glad they made the wise decision to move her family back to LA.

Roya speed dialed her mother. "Hey, Mom. I have two movie project offers from Mr. Johnson and Terry Perry."

"Roya, I'm so proud. Girl, that sounds wonderful. Do you think you can handle it with five children now?" She quizzed.

"Of course. Women do it all the time in Hollywood."

Jewel continued, "Yes they do. But your sons are capable of taking care of themselves."

"Okay."

"So, really you only need someone to look after the younger twins and keep your eye on my baby girl, Joy," Jewel added.

"Are you and Sunny willing to help me? I mean, watching my kids." Roya asked. She knew her mother stayed in Beverly Hills, but within proximity to help out.

"Of course. I think Sunny will have more time to do it since I'm franchising my business with other affiliated companies and e-commerce is booming this year!" Jewel yelled with glee.

"Oh, okay. Thanks for letting me know. I'll chat with Sunny later on this matter. Let me get back to the party." Roya disconnected the call. She blew hot air from her lips, thinking her mother always had a lame excuse when it came to her supporting and helping her eldest daughter but when her mother needed a favor Roya jumped to do it.

After the party had ended, Total Cleaning Service arrived on schedule to clean the home. Sondrea left a voice message that she'd return in a day or two. Roya prayed that

Sondrea would realize this isn't the life for her—preying on celebrities' wealth.

Chapter 21
Bitter instead of Better

JEWEL BATTLE

Beverly Hills
Jewel's Home

Jewel scrambled through her past mail. She slit the mail with a letter opener. She unfolded the letter. She carefully read the letter, but eyes darted at the Washington D.C. address. She presumed it was from Social Security Office. This was not the normal notification letter that came periodically. It was not AARP either. She re-read it a few times. She slammed the letter on the table.

She speed dialed Roya. The line rang four times before she was expecting voicemail to pick up. She heard a click.

"Mom," Roya answered.

She breathed heavily. "I cannot believe I got this crap in the mail."

"What in the mail?" Roya asked.

"The new administration office from Washington D.C. sent updated information about the pension and a separate letter about Social Security plans."

"Ok. So what is so bad about that?" Roya inquired.

"What's so *bad*?" Jewel yelled then removed the phone from her ear. She glanced at the cell for a moment to gather her thoughts and calm her temper.

"Yes, Mom. What? The administration office will stop dad's pension payments for some reason?" She guessed.

"Worse."

"What's worse?" Roya searched.

"For any retirement plans such as Social Security, stipulates that it will be mandatory to get chipped to receive your SSI. Pension payments are no longer sent by direct deposits to bank accounts or checks, but will have it on the chip as well."

"Whoa. I'm a bit confused." She gulped. "So you are saying that in order to get your monies, you have to be chipped?"

"Sounds right," Jewel said in frustration.

"This is *not* right."

"Exactly." Jewel snapped. "I have to comply within two months."

"What, go to one of those centers?"

"Yes." Jewel shook her head. "If I do not comply, I will not receive the pension or SSI benefits."

"Believe it or not, the schools are expecting the children to be chipped too. I got a letter not too long ago when I resided in Florida. So they are making these new laws to apply nationwide in the schools, which soon will be mandatory. Probably sooner, since you are getting this notice around the same time." Roya ranted.

"What are we going to do?" Jewel cried.

"Trust God. That may sound cliché, but His word says that He'll supply all our needs." Roya offered.

"Jesus. I can do all things through Christ who strengths me." Jewel added.

"Mom, know that I LOVE YOU."

"I love you too baby. Chat later." Jewel hung up the phone. Her frustration eased. She walked away from the notification letters.

❀SOLOMON❀

A couple of days passed. Solomon prepared his sermon for next Wednesday night's church service. Roya had to pick up the children from school in an hour. She yelled down the stairs, after getting out of the shower quickly and wrapped the white cotton towel around her naked body. Solomon had this evening's sermon ready.

Solomon hollered at the footstep to avoid climbing the stairs, "Honey, I'm fine. Are you dressed yet?"

The water bubbles drizzled down her legs as she wiped her body dry. Her forehead perspired while she dressed. She pressed the air conditioner button to HIGH. Solomon tapped his foot but no response from her. He staggered in the bathroom. Her body shook when he ambled, as he was an unsuspected guest in the room. Solomon chuckled at her sudden reaction.

"It's hot in here! You act like I've never seen you naked before."

"I know. I just thought you were someone else." She placed her hands over her breasts.

✝ 205

"Who else could it be? You're more nervous than I am tonight," Solomon said as he exited the bedroom. "I'll meet you at church," he called from downstairs.

❋ROYA❋

Roya flicked the switch to turn on the ventilating fan in the bathroom after slipping into her lavender sundress. She reached her fingers into the box of black bob pins as she pinned up her hair and put one at a time in her mouth until her hand was free to place another in her thick, kinky curls to stay in place. She dabbed the make-up brush in the powered reddish-toned blush onto her cheeks, then delicately drew across the dark-brown pencil over her eyebrows and brushed lightly over her eyelids a shimmering blue color to brighten her dark-brown eyes. Lastly, held her ruby lipstick in her right hand as the color glided over her puckered lips and smacked them twice for the color to blend nicely.

She sauntered out of the bathroom, raced down the stairs shoeless, and slipped into her purple sandal low-pump heels near the front door. She pushed the car keypad on her key change to start the engine and unlock the doors to her new Saturn mini-van. She whispered in frustration after walking away from the van, jingling the keys, opening the front door. "Dang, I always rush out and forget something."

Roya ran back inside the house to grab her leather case with Bible, journal, and iPad.

She froze in a stance when she heard familiar voices yelling. In the guest bedroom on the lower level with the door cracked wide open in her view where she stood motionlessly and her eyes glued on Sondrea as she crawled seductively on top of Solomon. He restrained her on the mattress and raced out of the room. Sondrea snickered and then stomped out of the room after him.

Sondrea screamed, "Solomon, you know that you want me. You need to quit playing with your emotions and swim in my ocean.

She patted below her waist when he glanced back. "I see the way you look at me! I see how you want to touch my body! Here I am, touch me!" She caressed her body with her hands and then licked her lips.

"Have you lost your darn mind?"

"Nope." She slurred. "I'm grown woman and know 'what she wants...she gets.'"

"You've been drinking." He yanked her hand. "Plus, I'm running late for an appointment. I need to stop and run a few errands before church. Another thing, are you out of your mind to try to do something with a married man in his own house!" Solomon fumbled and backed away from Sondrea as she aggressively reached out for him and didn't see his wife standing there before rushing out the front door.

Roya stood less than a few steps from the doorway. She wanted to cry but refused to shed a tear to mess up her mascara. She paused like she did when she caught Jaizon with Pamela. She saw clearly, that Sondrea slurred and wobbled—and she had to be drunk.

Roya wavered on sticking to the plan that she'd help Sondrea. Roya just stood like a mannequin and Sondrea didn't notice her. Roya mustered the strength to hide behind the closet door as Sondrea staggered back to the guest room and flopped on the bed. Roya heard Sondrea's groans—and the bed springs *zing*. She also heard Solomon's car engine start up and heard the whine of the engine as it faded in the distance.

She banged on the door of the guest room. "Sondrea," Roya yelled. "Get dressed; you're riding with me." She allowed the gospel tunes to soothe her mind while alone with Sondrea.

"Sondrea, come on. I'm ready to take you to put in for some jobs as I promised Mom."

"Jobs. Why would I do that?" Sondrea laughed heartily.

"Yes," Roya said.

"This is a joke, right? I have sung with Sunny on her album. I was to premiere in a movie project, remember?" Sondrea said sassily. She raised her hands.

"But I was thinking about tomorrow, most of the day, and wondering what you think about that," Roya continued, ignoring what she said.

Sondrea only shook her head in response.

"Although Mom has a home in Beverly Hills and in Florida, she wants you to be able to maintain and hold your own," Roya ratted.

"Whatever. She has enough money to take care of me. Why do I really have to work?" She snapped her finger. "This doesn't make any sense to me," Sondrea moped as she stepped into the car.

Roya puckered her lips and then followed a lopsided smile after listening to Sondrea's ungrateful remark while backing out of the garage. She refused to let on how she was feeling. She twitched her nose after smelling Sondrea's decayed-liquored breath, passing her a mint from her purse.

She swerved the steering wheel to make a U-Turn as Sondrea's body jerked and corner of her forehead bumped against the passenger window. Roya drove through a red light to turn in front of her children's school. Sondrea positioned and sat upright in the passenger seat. She crazily stared at Roya before making a remark.

"What the he—? Are you trying to kill us?" Sondrea's voice escalated an octave. She shook hysterically, breathing heavily and patted her chest.

"I should be asking you the questions. Let me pull over." She parked at the curb. "What the hell do you think you are doing with my husband?" Roya exclaimed.

"What do you mean?" Sondrea looked dumbfounded.

"I saw you all over Solomon in the guest bedroom. What's wrong with you?"

"What—"

"I allowed you to be in my home. I've been working with you to the best of my ability." She exhaled.

"You know what Sis, you're tripping." Sondrea turned her head and stared out the window.

"Yes, you're right about upcoming movie project you'll premiere in. But what will you do after that?" Roya barked. She was outraged and felt her hands easing from the steering wheel and visualized imprinting her fingerprints in Sondrea's neck after wringing the God-breathed life out of her. She gazed into her eyes, looking for sudden body movements, and to determine if she'd deny anything.

"First of all, no one put a gun to your head to let me in your home." Sondrea made a boom sound after making a gun hand gesture to her head.

Roya chuckled loudly and continued, "Honey-child—"

Sondrea motioned and unstrapped the seatbelt, "Now you believe you are helping me!"

"What the heck are you talking about?" Roya shook her head in disgust. "Geez, are you...kidding me," Roya profusely bluffed unadulterated cuss words without putting God's name in vain. Her heart raced rapidly.

Roya unstrapped her seatbelt as she glared outside the window to the heavens. "Come on now. What do you have to say for yourself? You're trying to avoid the question?" countered Roya, she felt like her head was on fire. She felt a tension headache after stressing over this mess. She rubbed her temples with her fingertips as Sondrea spoke.

"I'm not trying to avoid the darn question! You shouldn't be asking *me* this question! You know what. Let me out of this car!" Sondrea attempted to open the car door, but Roya had clicked the child-proof lock button.

"Not until you answer it truthfully," Roya asked again. She had her hand on the automatic button to keep her car doors locked.

"Yes, we made out once." Sondrea raised her forefinger. "Are you happy now!" She forced a fake smile. "I'm outta here," Sondrea lied and pressed the automatic unlock button.

"Shifting blame. OWN up!" Roya shouted.

Sondrea flung the passenger door open before Roya pushed the switch again. She jumped out and ran to the nearby streetlight.

Roya's cell phone rang seconds later. She answered the call. She refused to race after Sondrea saying, who slouched forward and skipped down sloped hill.

"Hello," She said as she watched Sondrea run to the streetlight a couple of blocks away from the school grounds.

"Hi, baby. I forgot my cufflinks. Can you bring them with you later on tonight at the meeting?" Solomon said.

"Ok." She caught her breath.

"Babe, I also left behind my notebook bag in the office at home that I'll be reading from at the Alliance Crusaders for Christ headquarters' meeting. I have my Bible, but I wanted to review my notes as well," said Solomon, impatiently.

Roya heard the wind hustling and traffic sounds coming from his end of the line. She pictured Solomon driving on the freeway with his windows cracked. She didn't respond to him but muted her phone, yelled and motioned Sondrea to come back. Sondrea ignored her and refused to look in her direction.

"You don't know where you're going? You're not from this city! Sondrea, get back in the car!"

"I'll find my way, Roya! I don't feel like talking about your *husband* right now. You probably won't believe me!"

"I'm not chasing after you!"

"I'll come back and pack my things to move back in Mom's house!" screamed Sondrea and jogged up the staircase of the metro transit bus.

Roya lost her reception on the cell phone once she entered the school building. The white plastic sign with bold red printed letters read, 'No cell phones are allowed. Please have them turned off before entering the building.' She pressed OFF on her mobile phone as instructed. Roya crept in Joy's classroom.

"Hi, Mommy!"

Joy was happy to see her mother as the school bell rang and rushed out the classroom door. She pulled her arms through her backpack and raced into Roya's arms. They walked next to the brick building where middle school students attended. Roya's heels click-clacked down the silent hallways, students still in their classes waiting for the bell to ring. She stopped at her son's homeroom and saw her elder boys in the classroom wearing three-dimensional headsets in which transform images into real-time while on their laptop computers. There are microprocessors used to coordinate the entire reality experience, controlling the lights, sound, and operation of the laser projectors with infrared signals that communicate to the headsets.

Other students had optical transmitters in their eyes, transparent and thin as a contact lens that beamed off their laptop computers. These students are in the school's biometric optical scanning system, and others had implanted biochips in their hands to use all school property equipment such as laptops, enter in school events, and eat school lunch. Those who refuse this biometric microchip implanting

✝ 212

process, still scan smart cards from the magnetic stripe read all their school information, and use of the wireless laptop computers in the classrooms and usage of the digital libraries.

Joy peeked inside and gritted her teeth when one of her brothers glanced at the glass windowed wooden door. The buzz of the bell rang through the hallways. The boys ran to the door after the ringing sounds of the bell and noticed their mother's eyes piercing through the class window.

"Mrs. Whitmore, I'd like to talk to you in private, before you leave," Mrs. Bellington shuffled papers off her desk into her large handbag and stuffed her laptop inside before zipping it.

"I'm sort of in a rush," Roya said, breathing heavily.

"This will not take long. Please?" Mrs. Bellington said.

"Okay, what is this about, Mrs. Bellington?" Roya groped.

"I'd like to advance your sons to a higher grade level. They've taken tests that show their scores are at college level. I've spoken to the principal too."

"Ok, this is great." Her eyes lit up.

"But there is a problem, as you may know."

"What might that be, Mrs. Bellington?" Her voice deepened.

"The school policy is changing rapidly. Since most of the parents agreed to the biochip and the updated technology administered reads the chip for lunch programs, classrooms are digitally reading the chip for attendance, and so forth," Mrs. Bellington said, taking a breath. Then she continued,

"Well, um, it will be mandatory to continue in school functions," Mrs. Bellington's voice lowered to a whisper.

"Whoa. Slow down. I got the letter not too long ago, but that was in Florida."

"Also taking place here in California..." the teacher offered.

"So are you telling me they are forcing our children to insert the chip to get school lunches, for attendance purposes, etcetera?"

"This is correct."

"When does this take place?"

"Soon. Real soon." She stared into Roya's eyes. A teacher entered the room. Mrs. Bellington went back on topic, "We'll call you to setup a conference meeting or virtual meeting on SKYPE at your convenience to converse further on this matter with the principal to see what best suits your needs and your children."

"Ok." Roya's eyes darted at both teachers in the room. She caught the signals and why Mrs. Bellington changed the topic as soon as this female teacher entered the room.

"I've also spoken with the admission counselors of nearby colleges. You have time to decide and expect to hear from us in a week to schedule an appointment to meet with me, the principal and the admission counselors."

"I see that you are busy. I'll chat with you later." The female teacher said before exiting the room.

Mrs. Bellington paused for a moment until the woman left. She whispered, "I'll also be at that church revival tonight. I'd love to hear your husband preach tonight."

"Oh yes, that reminds me why I was in a rush to leave."

"I am sorry I held you longer than you anticipated. But think about what I said."

"Between you and I, my children will be homeschooled before getting chipped."

"I understand perfectly." Mrs. Bellington said.

"Interesting. Thank you for this information, Mrs. Bellington. I have to be leaving now," Roya responded as she stepped further away from the door.

Mrs. Bellington waved good-bye to the boys as they looked back.

Roya knew her darling little princess was growing into a young lady. Joy had turned ten, looking at least twelve years old. She shook her head at the thought of the years whooshed like a vapor. She exits the front doors with her children as other students rammed out of the doors, chattering and whistling, and school buses at posted areas. She knew she had to make another pit-stop at the babies' daycare. Roya and her three children climbed the hill to the get to the mini-van parked on the street. A traffic patrol officer parked behind the car, indicating that she was parking in a school zone area, and was printing out a ticket off his compact wireless printer.

"Officer, I'm terribly sorry. I won't park here anymore." She raised her hands. "I'm already at my van and will gladly move it, sir." She grabbed her keys out of her purse. "Please forgive me. I'm leaving as we speak once I got all of my children in the van." Roya pleaded and opened the driver's side, stood there in hopes he'd rip the ticket in small pieces.

"I'll let it pass this time!" patrol officer responded nonchalantly.

"Thank you, officer." She whooshed. "What a day."

"Next time, whether or not you run out to your van in the future, this ticket meter will print off a ticket."

"What do you mean, officer?" She pressed the button to start the engine.

"Now, we're creating meters with voice command that'll read off your ticket information and the computer automatically in your computerized vehicles until it's paid in full."

"So how will we pay it? With our biochip?" She teased.

He continued regardless of the interruption. "We'll allow drivers to add a device to pay their tickets by pressing a button in their cars." He answered.

"A device will be installed in our vehicles to make a payment for tickets," Roya repeated, deadpan.

"I'll be glad because it makes my job easier! No more trailing cars down for tickets and printing them out on this darn machine!"

"Ok." She envisioned the device installed in the cars and with the swipe of the hand, showed on the computer screen paid in full.

"Also, we have surveillance cameras setup on every block, snapping pictures and license plates, so people can't talk their way out of tickets!"

"Yes, I've seen the cameras."

"Just a warning ma'am, that'll occur within the next month or two. You should receive something in the

✝ 216

electronic mail or on your mobile IM service from Digital Motor Vehicles." He explained and nodded his head as he walked to his traffic vehicle.

Roya nodded and thanked him with a smile. She was overwhelmed after hearing about this new digital system to make jobs easier, efficient, and less labor from employees. She glanced at her keys, and then her eyes darted at her children, unable to imagine a chip in each of them. Once she drove off the school site, she phoned the daycare provider to inform the teacher that she was running behind schedule. After loading the babies, she drove to the nearest fast food restaurant to feed her family. She pulled in the drive-thru at Galaxy McDonald's instead of going to New Saturn's Restaurant. Each child yelled out what they wanted on the menu, heard on the intercom and rang up their order on the screen and paid for the food via credit card. The drive-thru worker handed her food and drinks; then she drove off after handing their bags to them to eat in the car during the drive. She made one more stop at home to get the what-not's Solomon asked for and let the kids change out of their school uniforms into church clothes.

Roya nibbled on her food while driving to the church. Her fries were cold and greasy, drink watered down, and surprisingly the chicken sandwich was lukewarm. She threw the remaining food away. She arrived at the church at 4:30 p.m. But Roya couldn't get those images of Sondrea and Solomon out of her mind. She parked the car, seemed distant and aloof, but the kids hopped out of the van. Her sons unstrapped the twins, and each carried one while their mother slid out of her seat and locked the doors by the push of a button on the keychain.

Solomon posted at the main door entrance to grab the iPad from Roya's hand after she took it out of the book bag. The kids followed their father inside of the church hallway. She placed the sleeping babies in the twin-set baby stroller after the boys handed them over to her one by one before trotting down the hallway of the church. Solomon wanted to say something like, 'What took you so long?' But he saw that Roya was occupied and left to put his things under the podium.

Roya sauntered down the aisle until she reached the front of the pulpit where her children were sitting, anticipating hearing their father preach at this headquarter meeting. Church members and new recruits were finding a place to sit before the event begun. She lowered her head, eyes not looking at him because of her discomfiture at Sondrea.

Solomon stood at the altar, wireless microphone attached to his suit. A video camera with virtual screens while speaking would allow Internet viewers to see the entire video screening on real-time. He eagerly shared the prophetic truth. Their children were quiet and attentive, hanging on every word their father spoke. Roya was proud of her children, so mannerly and showed respect for the speaker while in the special church service. She was praising God silently that Solomon Junior and Selena were still asleep. She had the milk and juice in an ice pack to stay chilled until time for their feeding in Sippy cups.

Isaiah introduced Solomon Whitmore, "Solomon will share what the Lord Jesus has placed on his heart and mind."

Roya heard Isaiah and realized this wasn't a special headquarters' meeting as she was advised earlier on the phone call.

❋SOLOMON❋

Solomon stepped up to the platform to start his lesson. "Thank you, Pastor, Isaiah." He lightly clapped and nodded at Isaiah before starting his sermon.

"We need to get out of our comfort zones and believe we're in control of our lives. At times, it may seem or appear like we are, but God is our Creator and looks at us. God's knowledge and wisdom are far greater than man's." He cleared his throat. He sipped on his bottled water.

He stared into his wife's brown eyes. "Patience allows love, which is a desire to benefit from one another at your own expense, to become the preeminent force in the relationship. Love holds a relationship together: not infatuation, attraction, or even desire." He then glanced at the other members as he spoke with elegance. "We're *missing the mark*, which is a biblical term for messing with God's perfect plan or living a life in sin."

"Okay." Roya looked toward the shout to see a woman nodding in agreement.

"Forgive me for a moment, but the Lord Jesus is taking me another direction. We will touch more on the *mark of the beast.*"

✝ 219

"Preach." A man shouted.

"Mark of the Beast is a layman term concerning the man who will come as if he is the Messiah and wants his loyal followers to have his mark that shows you are following the way."

"Teach." Another member responded.

"Jesus said, "I am the way, the truth, and the light. But the imposter, also known as the Antichrist, will come as the Messiah, delivering his *way, his truth,* which many will follow, and will impress many that his message is the light but only a deception of his cunningness."

He raised his finger while reading his sermon notes. "What is this deception? He is using the peace we have longed for as a ruse to make us believe this method of chipping humans is our answer. Supposedly, they'll say, *'We have true safety and security in technology. Satellites are placed in space, and can watch people in real time. Already watching us with the cameras posted on the street lights and other buildings, including drones.'* But with the *chip* inserted in our bodies, biochemists show that it will also conform our minds to follow the leader's way. We'd become like him." He carefully defined.

"If there are no boundaries, once we are chipped and we become susceptible to Satan's perversion, we will be trapped. We are tracked. We are watched. We are being transformed into the Devil's image once we take his mark..." He loosened the collar on his shirt and picked up his handkerchief from his breast pocket to wipe the sweat from his brow.

"How is this happening? For example, my children have been required to take the chip. The first incident occurred when my wife gave birth to our other set of twins. They expected her to sign, immediately, a form giving consent to insert the chip in our babies. She refused, which was her right. Then she signed the proper form to apply for a birth certificate."

He continued after glancing at his wife and her angry face, "Now our teen sons and daughter, Joy, have been required at their schools to sign a consent form that came from the Administration Office in D.C. to insert the chip in order to eat school lunches, go to special events, and just to go through the secured entrance doors. And my wife told me the other night that her mother cannot get her pension check unless she conforms to the new administration laws of getting chipped. This is taking place nationwide within months."

"Tell us, Pastor." Someone said.

"So we strongly need a relationship with God and ability to hear His voice in this hour." He pointed at his chest. "Prayer is intimacy with God, not quick answers." He raised his prayer hands. "Let's read from John 15:5. Be prepared to act on it and desire to know and do all for the will of God."

"Yes, we do need to know God's will in his hour," Roya shouted.

"God's willing to make His purpose known—not show it unless you're considering doing it. God desires to develop you and what He plans to do things your life. Submit your situation to Jesus."

✝ 221

"Amen." A few shouted in unison.

"We will be called 'rebels' or even 'terrorists' because we follow the way of Jesus." He surveyed the crowd and saw the attentiveness of the members, eyes glued on the projector screen when the scripture appeared as he read it. He dabbed the handkerchief on his forehead.

"My wife and I discussed in brief that the government will rely on the military if not already, known as martial law." He raised his head to the heavens and then lowered his head, pushing aside his notes.

"What is it, Minister?" a male urged.

"I strongly believe that this new leader will make us *all* take the mark through an executive order by demanding *us* to take the biochip implant." He touched his chest in reference to *us* and then pointed at the members in the crowd. "Give me a moment to give you a brief outline on martial law." He rushed to type in the URL after clicking the Internet to locate the meaning of martial law on the Web.

"Help us Minister Whitmore." Someone shouted.

"Martial Law means using the state or national military force to enforce the will of the government on the people. Our constitutional freedoms and liberties are suspended and lose our civil rights. Furthermore, martial law will impose its will through military force."

"Jesus help us." A member exclaimed.

"Everything is done with God's help, but God helps those who help themselves."

"Alright, Pastor."

"Martial law is nothing new under the sun. America took hold of this method in the Revolutionary war. The main catalyst was the English men who used the military troops to enforce everyday law throughout the colonies. Then flash forward to the Civil War. These atrocities were committed by President Lincoln. History repeats itself, and when the man is in power, we'll be imposed with also a Congressionally-authorized martial law if not already in progress." He knew he was long-winded but had more to share with the crowd.

"Be prepared when they call it a 'State of an Emergency' and I strongly believe there will be mandatory curfews, mandatory identifications at checkpoints, automatic search and seizures no longer abiding by the Fourth Amendment." He wiped his mouth. "Furthermore, travel restrictions like road closures. Quarantine believers in these concentration camps to take the mark or else you will lose your head."

"What can we do Pastor?"

"Pray." Someone responded.

"We will have to learn to be equipped spiritually as well as mentally." He paused.

He turned to a passage in the Bible, "Romans 12:2 clearly tells us not to conform to the ways of this world but to be transformed by the renewing of our minds. Then we can test and approve what God's will is—his good, pleasing and perfect will."

"Preach to us."

"We have to think on our toes. For instance, God has given me dreams of these soldiers driving in tanks like it is a war ahead, or 28-foot moving vans...coming by the load in uniform, barring in people's homes or living spaces, and forcing them out. Those who refuse will be gunned down in the streets and their blood will spill for all to see." He noticed Roya's uneasiness while teaching this lesson. He couldn't keep his eyes off of her every time he looked her way while speaking to the crowd.

"Jesus!" someone shouted in fright.

Roya crossed her legs and hands still folded, easing forward and nearly out of her seat. He could clearly see that she wondered where his lesson was going with this by the quizzical look cast on her face.

He brushed through the lesson and glared at the clock rested on his stand, "Joshua is our computer and technology specialist who have already created devices to keep us alert with the Special Operations, military, and even the drones. Josh and Yosef have been working on solar vehicles that do not need gas to operate or function, but fuel with corn oil or even water. I have already stored tons of food for when we are unable to buy or sell."

"Praise God."

"I am hearing the Pharaoh's dream. I have had the dreams and our team is already moving forward to do what we need to do to survive. We need to allow Jesus to direct us."

As Jesus said in John 18 verse 36, "His kingdom is not of this world." Our happiness is in Paradise with him in the Heavenly skies!" He exclaimed with excitement. The crowd cheered except for his wife.

❋ROYA❋

Roya continued to have flashbacks. Her wet armpits left a showing circle on her gray-ruffled blouse and felt a slight wet stain on the backside of her pantsuit from perspiration. Her bladder was full and eager to release but wanted to hear the ending of his lesson. Solomon's sermon touched Roya towards the closing stages.

He stepped off the podium and Isaiah closed with next meeting announcements. Afterward, Roya watched her husband and Isaiah step into a secluded room before leaving that night. Then, he spoke with a few members about his sermon while Roya and the family waited nearby. Solomon told Roya he would stay a few more minutes. She drove the kids' home in the mini-van.

Chapter 22
Spying for the Truth

ROYA WHITMORE

Florida

The following week, Roya had to settle some matters in her hometown back in Florida. She felt unction to make a stop near her home. But she was stopped by her next door neighbor. When Diamond opened the side door, she wanted to say something except her neighbor spoke first.

"There's something I need to tell you," Diamond said with urgency.

"What's up, Diamond?" Roya squinted her eyes.

"You know how we've became close and I thought you have a right to know this information," said Diamond.

"Yeah, we are close. I'll be doing a short sermon tomorrow night," said Roya after looking around the corner of her shoulder.

"Okay. I saw that sister of yours with your husband. I have it on camera if you'd like to view it. I made a copy on micro-diskette on DVD-RW. Here. We can talk about it when you get a chance," said Diamond, handing over the disk to Roya.

"Um. Interesting. You would have something like this on hand. I'd definitely like to see this." Roya decided she would share more information with her neighbor than she expected. "I tried to talk to her and she stepped out of my car."

"Really?"

"She wouldn't admit if she was responsible for it. I saw them with my own eyes walking down the stairs, but Solomon left."

"So you know?" asked Diamond, shaking hysterically, directing Roya inside.

Roya took a seat where Diamond stood with the remote in her hand to press "play." The miniature DVD clearly displayed Sondrea, in the house drunk as Solomon carried her inside when the fiasco took place. He placed her in the bed. Sondrea puckered her lips to place kisses on his cheeks, and then imprinting lipstick kisses of her lips on his cheeks, forehead, and on his lips. The dark room made it difficult to make out any other details. However, Roya saw Sondrea's arms wrap around Solomon's neck, and trying to tongue-kiss him. He murmured foreign words, and then Sondrea sat upright in the bed. Then, she fell back, and undressed herself slowly. She reached and tugged at Solomon's black polyester pants. And then, she reached for his legs, trying to entwine him in a sexual act.

"You know that you're feeling me. You know how I watched your manhood rise for me last time. All I did was touch you. We can do so much in the dark. I'm a little nervous, but I know that you're the one that I want to have

✝ 227

my all. Let's make it right, I want to sex you all night! No condoms. Let's not waste time so I feel you inside of me...I can make love to you," Sondrea slurred the words 'make love to you' as she tugged at his black blazer.

"Are you crazy? I have a wife, who is your sister Roya." Solomon snapped, trying to get away from Sondrea.

"Correction, she's my half-sister. I hardly even know Roya. It's not like we grew up with each other. I want to get to know you better though, sexy chocolate," begged Sondrea.

After she clumsily unbuckled his pants, Solomon pulled them back at his waist line and attempted to leave the room. Sondrea fell out of the bed, trying to place her head below his belt, and he pushed her head back and staggered out of the room.

This incident was recorded on July 4th at 3:00 a.m. Roya carefully calculated precisely the dates of these sexual advances recorded on her home recorder from the secretly hidden miniature cams and Diamond's recording. Then, dated two weeks later, Sondrea attempted to throw herself on Solomon in his office room, reminding him of the incident she was drunk and that she was willing to tell Roya. Sondrea promised to make it more than meets the eyes.

After Roya asked Diamond to pause the DVD, she pressed PAUSE on the player and voice-commanded the television to turn OFF.

"Diamond," Roya said, "Thank you. You are a true friend. I already knew that Sondrea was being a brat, for lack of a better way to say it. This proves to me that my husband has been faithful."

"Are you crazy? How in the world did he get in the same room with that girl?"

"Look," Roya sighed. "That girl is drunk, dumb and would do anything to create a problem if she thought it would get her ahead. Solomon is doing the right thing. Right now, we've got more pressing issues. Sondrea needs our Lord. Would you pray with me?"

Diamond looked dubious, but reluctantly grabbed Roya's hands and bowed her head.

"Lord, please help us keep our minds stayed on You. There are demons out to get those we love, and our precious children, and keep in from your gracious care. Thank You, Lord. In Jesus' name, Amen."

Diamond gave her the DVD to review later if she needed, and left.

Sondrea needs to leave our house.

When Roya arrived back home, she placed the DVD on the counter in the living room. Jewel sauntered in and glared at Roya.

"Mom. What are you doing here?"

"I'm glad you even noticed me. What has been going on with you lately?" Jewel quizzed with concern.

"Well, I got an offer from Terry already for a movie project and he wants me to fly down right away. Why would that be a problem?" She answered cautiously. She hoped her mother would offer to stay with the kids.

Neither of them realized Solomon stepped in but paused in his tracks as he stood within earshot of their mother-daughter confab.

"I'll have to check with Solomon to see how the music production offers are going."

"Okay..."

"I think Sondrea has to touch bases with him too, oops. I didn't mean to mention her name after what happened!" Roya said.

"What you mean? You didn't *mean* to mention her?" Jewel folded her arms. Her head titled to the side.

"I gave Sondrea a shot and don't think she will work out. She has outdone her welcome." Roya stormed off.

Jewel turned and saw Solomon. "So you heard. You in agreement with my headstrong daughter?"

"Yes, Mama. That vixen's been trying to get me to bed her and she drinks like the Pacific Ocean is full of booze. You don't have any idea what she is capable of doing." He made hand gestures of smoking and drinking, giving googly eyes. "I'm glad Roya's seeing the light. But don't you go telling Roya anything I said tonight, because you know how Roya gets upset at such things. She's a good mama to my kids, and I love her." He patted his chest.

Chapter 23
God Only Knows What's in Store

SOLOMON WHITMORE

Los Angeles, CA
Mansion Home

Solomon came home at 10:00 p.m. He noticed Roya sitting in the living room, watching the Gospel Channel and flipping to see what was on The Word Christian channel.

"Solomon, is that you?"

"Yes."

"Can you come here for a minute? I'd like to ask you something." Roya voice heightened in suspension.

"Sure. I'd like to get something to drink from the refrigerator first." He walked in the other direction to the kitchen before heading into the living room. The dimness of the lightening in the room told him that the children were sleep, and she was either upset about something or had a sensual appetite.

"Okay," said Roya.

Minutes later, he entered the living room, and she said, "I'm scared. I've tried to hold up, but honestly, Solomon, I've been having an awful time, worrying about the way things are going in this world."

Tears ran down her cheeks.

She continued, "I have faith in Jesus. I trust the Lord."

"Then what is troubling you, dear." Solomon's face softened, and he welcomed his wife to his chest.

"I'm scared. Did we make the right decision to move to LA? It seems like they have been doing the chipping here too? California is known for strict rules and adapting to such measures as well as Florida." Roya cried.

"It can be frightening. I couldn't believe we had to sign paperwork to reject the chipping for the babies. This has never been requested or happened before. But we should not be surprised since it is in the Holy Word. We need to be ready, watchful and pray."

She rose up and stared into his brown eyes nervously, "Ready...pray! These are our children we are talking about. The government is going too far to expect newborn babies to get chipped. Kids in school to get chipped. The twins are older and can comprehend, but Joy is putting the pieces together...what will we do?"

"Not what we will do, but trust God and what He will tell us to do. Trust your visions. Trust that He will speak to us in due time. I have been putting some things together to make sure our family is secure when matters worsen."

Her hands twitched. Her eyes filled with tears. "Worsen. Maybe we should hide..."

"Hide? You are scared. You are not thinking and waiting on the Lord for answers. We are seeing things before our eyes to convince us believers that the time is near, but we have to be mindful how we react to Satan's attacks."

"You're right. God would never leave us nor forsake. He will show us a way of escape." She nodded nervously and then rested on her husband's chest as his arms enveloped her and held her close.

"Now, Roya," he said after she'd calmed a bit. She looked up at him. "I've got to go on some business. I promise I'm not going to do anything to hurt you or the kids, but all this stuff is worrying you, it's bothering us, too."

"No, Sol, please, not now."

"I'll leave in the morning."

❀ROYA❀

Late the next evening, Roya sat in tears as she listened to the news. She switched to the preachers but was still too upset. She felt ill and headed to the bathroom.

A stern voice spoke to Roya's mind, and she felt a chilling spirit move over her. *'My child, this is unbelief. If you can only trust Me, I'll show you what's to come.'*

She opened her Bible to read Genesis 15:1, *"Fear not, Abram: I am your shield and your exceedingly great reward."* She placed her Bible back on the shelf behind the toilet. The Lord spoke to her spirit again after she read the scripture, *'I am your shield through any discouragement, misery, hurt, pain, for protection, and you shall see your reward if you totally believe and trust in Me. I can increase your faith through tests and trials. Pick up your Bible that's on the back shelf behind your toilet and allow your fingers to turn to the Scripture I want you to read.'*

1

1

Adrienna Turner

She was obedient to the voice of the Lord. She reached upward to pick up the Bible again. Her hands shook uncontrollably, and her body suddenly felt relieved from all her problems and troubles. The weight of sin burdening her was lifted, and her tears spilled over with joy. She turned the pages, and her fingers stopped on James 1. Her heart was touched deeply as she read aloud softly, *"Consider it pure joy, my brothers and sisters, whenever you face trials of many kinds because you know that the testing of your faith produces perseverance. Let perseverance finish its work so that you may be mature and complete, not lacking anything."*

She read below in her Study Bible to get a clearer explanation of this scripture. It read, *"We can't really know the depth of our character until we see how we react under pressure. It is easy to be kind to others when everything is going well, but can we still be kind when others are treating us unfairly? God wants to make us perfect and complete, not to keep us from all pain. Instead of complaining about our struggles, we should see them as opportunities for growth. Thank God for promising to be with you in rough times. Ask Him to help you solve your problems or to give you the strength to endure them. Then be patient, God will not leave you alone with your problems; He will stay close and help you grow."*

God also directed Roya to turn to Proverbs 4:23-27, as she read, *"Keep your heart with all diligence, for out of it spring the issues of life. Put away from you a deceitful mouth, and put perverse lips far from you. Let your eyes look straight ahead, and your eyelids look right before you. Ponder the paths of your feet, and let your ways be*

✝ 234

established. Do not turn to the right or to the left; Remove your feet from evil." These words spoke to her heart and mind with discernment. *"Our heart—our feelings of love and desire—dictates to a great extent how we live because we always find time to do what we enjoy. King Solomon tells us to guard our heart above all else, making sure we concentrate on those desires that will keep us on the right path. Make sure your affections push you in the right direction. Put boundaries on your desires: do not go after everything you see. Look straight ahead, keep your eyes fixed on your goal, and don't get sidetracked on detours that lead to sin."*

Roya realized what God was showing her. She needed to make some changes in her life. She had internal issues with mothering her children. She had to focus on the goal God had for her life and not to get sidetracked with ill-gotten desires. Then, she asked God, "Thank you, Lord, for showing me what you needed to let me see. I ask for forgiveness and those who I've hurt. Please Lord; allow me to do Your will and not my own. Amen."

Roya rinsed her face and minor scratches on her arms with Witch Hazel and stepped out of the bathroom. She checked on her children in the game room. Joy had fallen asleep on the couch with the television still on. Tavon and Javon jumped up when they saw their mother's presence in the room. She ignored their mumbles.

"Just sit down. Better yet, go back to sleep like Joy did. We can discuss this later. This is grown folks business. I know you're my eldest kids, but you need to stay in a child's place!" Roya said to Tavon after he inquired about why his mother and dad weren't together.

"Where's Dad?" Tavon pushed, licking his lips.

"He's out on another business trip!" Roya's voice exploded and then she left the game room.

Tavon and Javon stood speechless. Obviously, sadness filled their spirits after their mother raised her voice. She entered the kitchen after Sunny had changed the twins' Pull-Ups and dumped them in the trash.

"How are you girl?" asked Sunny.

"I guess okay."

Sunny tilted her head. "You sure?"

"Yea. Sondrea bragged that he owes her money and condo or some crap. I'll have to find out about that. Did he offer you the same?" Roya remained cordial.

"I'm not sure. I have an agent and will check with her. Um, your little ones, Selena and Junior fell asleep after they ate, and I was shocked they didn't get up to go potty. So I changed their pull-ups. I'll put them back to bed, and we can talk afterwards," Sunny explained.

"Sunny, don't worry about it. You look exhausted, and it's early in the morning, like close to one a.m. We can talk later, though," Roya replied. She sat down with a cup of hazelnut coffee, sipping on it until Jewel entered.

"The truth shall set you free. I've brought Sondrea back in the room to admit the truth," Jewel pushed Sondrea into the kitchen.

"Mother, it's too late."

"The girl has something to say to you, and you're going to listen!" Jewel said. Her 'don't argue with me' voice told Roya all.

"Mom, I mean...Jewel's right. I was wrong. I was drunk and didn't know what I was doing. Solomon was nice enough to come pick me up after I was stranded at a Fourth of July party at some club. I'm sorry, Ro-Ro. Come on Roya. Can you forgive me or accept my apology?" Sondrea whined. She inched closer to Roya, who leaned against the island in the kitchen.

Roya glared at her. "Not good enough, Girl," she said. "I know the truth. I just want to hear it from your mouth minus the sass!"

Sondrea moseyed closer at a slower pace, "Ok, I will admit that I made advances to him at the studio and in the house a couple days later. But, believe me when I say this, that man of yours...he really loves you." She sighed and raved about him, "You're blessed to have a man like Solomon. I pray for a man like him! I'd do anything to have him or someone like him. He's a provider, husband, father, and faithful man. He's a God-fearing man too. He also is a music producer, actor and producing his own movies and other televised shows. I wished I had all that. I envied you. I wanted what you had, which I shouldn't have tried to take away from you," cried Sondrea, taking baby steps closer to the island in the center of the kitchen where Roya was sitting. Her face reddened as Roya's face became blandly pale. Jewel patted Sondrea on the back lightly.

Roya thought, *God works in mysterious ways especially since I'm supposed to ask Sondrea for forgiveness.*

"Oh okay. Thanks for sharing that. I'm glad to know that my man wasn't coming on to you as you indicated before. Oh well, he's gone now. I forgive you," Roya said. *She doesn't need to know Solomon and I are okay. Let the girl stew a bit. It'll be good for her.*

"Thank you. I forgive you too. I sure don't want to rot in Hell for this." Sondrea looked at Jewel as she nodded her head and then at Roya. Roya just looked away and sipped on her coffee again, smiling inside.

"Do I still need to move out?" asked Sondrea.

"I think its best. Mom said you could live with her. You're set and blessed. Don't mess it up with Mom again, 'cause those bridges won't be easily fixed. Not saying that Mom isn't a forgiving and loving person, just that she'll hold grudges a great deal longer than I do. Remember, I'm older, and I lived with her my whole life!" Roya said, looking at Jewel with a twinkle in her eye. "Right now, I need to take heed to what he said to me earlier today!" Roya admitted and looked upward.

Jewel kissed Roya on the cheek, hugged her, and said her farewells. Sondrea also hugged and kissed Roya. Jewel and Sondrea packed Sondrea's things and left the house.

Epilogue
Jehovah Shalom

SOLOMON WHITMORE

Los Angeles, CA
Mansion Home

Solomon arrived home a week later. The house seemed dark and settled. He heard the television blaring from the living room. He drew closer and placed the luggage near the stairway. He breathed easily and slipped into the living room. His chest rose as he glared at the television screen.

"Special report. We have startling news that is happening worldwide. What is causing these atrocities?" The news anchor tried to remain calm, but her eyes flashed with fear and terror. "Japan has had massive killings that have not happened in centuries. The United States has had police brutalities, massive shootings to those who are innocent, and fires here in California. In Chile, there were massive earthquakes and even in Baja, Mexico. There have been frequent hurricanes in the Southern States." She paused as she glanced at her iPad on the podium. The camera flashed some of the disasters the news anchor touched on as a camera person pointed at the prompter.

"Baby, what are you doing up this hour?" Solomon said as he sat next to his wife.

"Waiting up for you." She eased into a smile.

"What time is it?" He glanced at his Rolex. "It is past 1 a.m. Did you have one of your dreams?"

"You know I am a night owl..." Roya showed him her lopsided smile.

"I know that look. Wait, is that Isaiah Williams?" Solomon's eyes widened and pointed in the direction of the television screen.

She nodded.

"I can answer what is going on with these catastrophes you spoke about earlier." Isaiah offered. He wore a silver Armani suit, matching silver and black striped tie, black handkerchief in the pocket slit and lightly pressed black shirt. He sat upright with confidence and his eyes glimmered with hope. He wore freshly cut hair and clasped his fingers as he eloquently answered the questions until another guest arrived on the set.

"These are episodes mentioned by the writer John, who was the beloved disciple of Jesus Christ. He predicted these very apocalyptic events that would let believers know that the time is near."

"The time is near?" The anchor repeated, looking at Isaiah with shock.

"Yes. To prepare for the tribulation. Jesus spoke to us in John chapter 16 verse 33: 'I have told you these things so that in me you may have peace. In this world, you will have trouble. But take heart! I have overcome the world.'" Isaiah stated.

"You expect us to believe this nonsense?" A man, dressed in a white robe strode in, with Hebrew Slavic garb dangling around his neck and hanging down to his knees. He spoke with a voice of authority. "These disasters are occurring because of the global warming; the ground is breaking open due to seismic rationale which is caused by earthquakes or the vibration of the earth due to natural causes. The killings and shootings are evident due to hate-filled men and women today."

"Thank you for sharing that, Prime Minister Hadrianus," the female news anchor said graciously. "I must confess to not feeling all that comforted by your news."

"I have also brought the Lieutenant Les Blanche with me this evening." Prime Minister held his hand in the direction where Les was stepping on the platform.

"Is this a pre-recorded show?" Solomon interrupted.

Roya nodded, turning to Solomon, her eyes wide.

"Thank you, Mrs. Childers, for welcoming us on the show this evening."

"Tell us your position on these catastrophes, atrocities, and disasters we are experiencing," she spoke quickly.

"As a military leader, we suggest that the public abides by the new regulations and laws that are passed. To be within compliance, follow orders, and the purpose of the Task Force is to enforce these laws with the abiding citizens. We are assisting the police force, FBI, CIA, and other adjunction agencies to get other citizens in compliance with these laws. We are doing everything we can to protect and serve, but more importantly, to see peace again in the world." Les sternly offered.

"How do these new laws help with those atrocities we covered at the top of the hour?"

"We have to have rules and laws to keep things in order. Once things are out of order, we see crimes occur more rapidly, such as shooting sprees. We see and experience chaos. Murders. We have to enforce these rules, regulations, and comply with administrative laws in each state." He spoke without compassion or concern. His voice remained stern and firm. He stared at the news anchor and would not look at Isaiah, but took a few glances at Prime Minister, who would give a slight nod or side smile. "We already have advised abiding citizens to get chipped. We have seen how people are transitioning into this new system in place and becoming peaceful, unified group."

"So you are justifying *unity* for the community…?" Mrs. Childers added, "But all this is happening at once, and earthquakes have never been known to follow a law."

"I see through this military-law-abiding routine. I know who you work for and who you are!" Isaiah spoke as he rose from his studio seat. He crossed his hand over his other hand, making a *cross* symbol and spoke in a foreign tongue.

The studio went dark; camera shot a spark of light, and the room shook before the program stopped airing.

There was a dark screen and loud annoying buzz stayed on the television for thirty seconds. Roya reached for the remote and shut the television off. The loud annoying noise woke up her older children; Tavon, Javon, and Joy.

"Dad. Mom." Tavon and Javon said in unison.

"What was that alarming noise?" Joy screeched, covering her ears.

"I turned it off." Roya rose from her seat and welcomed her children with open arms.

"This is a time to pray. I am glad you were awakened. We saw something quite disturbing on the news at this hour." Solomon said firmly. His eyes glistened.

"Dad…is it what you have been warning us about?" Tavon, the eldest son, asked.

"Yes my firstborn. It is the breaking of the tribulation. We have witnessed the *sign of the times* with the rumor of wars. Earthquakes. Massive killing and shootings are occurring worldwide. These newsworthy stories and incidents have never occurred simultaneously until now." Solomon said as he fell to his knees in the middle of the living room. Roya knelt gracefully beside him. Their children encircled them.

"You kids are important to me. I need us all to survive in these trying times. Know that I love each and every one of you dearly," Roya said, kissing each one of them on their forehead. She clasped her husband's hand.

He took hold of his eldest son's hand, Tavon, and lifted it in the air. "I pray for you, my son. I also pray for you, Javon. You are the *two voices* in this hour. You will preach the message to the youth. Join hands now."

The sons obeyed and held hands together, fervently praying until they spoke in the Hebrew tongue. Solomon's soul rang peace and direction as the Holy Spirit spoke silently to him. He shook his head in agreement with the Spirit. Roya spoke firmly, "Lord, we have seen your servant Isaiah with the Prime Minister from Rome and militant leader Les, and please protect Isaiah in this hour. We have witnessed your power on the broadcast and the evil at work. We pray you shut down every evil plan of the enemy and

✝ 243

open the windows of heaven to surround your angels to every saint to protect and direct our path for what to do in this hour. I pray for a touch from you right now. Touch my children with your Holy presence."

Joy softly prayed, "Yahweh, Jesus, Father God, please bless this household. Bless my parents. Bless us in this hour. We stand in the need of prayer and guidance. God, I know you are here. Bless your Holy name, Jesus. Amen."

Solomon cried. He hugged each member of his family. He checked on his toddlers, resting in their beds, and planted a kiss on each one of them with a silent prayer. 'YWHH will not forsake us,' he whispered. 'I will uphold the plans you have spoken and carry out your will for you and my family. Jesus, your will be done. Amen.'

Author's Commentary

While writing this novel, I was led by the Holy Spirit in 2005. At the end of 2006, I started to gather ideas and geared into writing this action-packed story.

In this book, I quote from scriptures, discuss biblical principles and recount events that are destined to occur as described in Revelation, Daniel, and John's Visions in 1 John. Additionally, there are descriptions of dreams and visions from the author to demonstrate what will transpire soon. There are fictional characters to enlighten you as to events coming according to God's Holy Word. This book also reveals symbolic and futuristic events.

For example, Genesis 1 refers to the beginning and a world in darkness and without form and void. Today, our world is still in darkness without God's Word and caught up into worldly things (carnal mind and beliefs), no morals and void of anything that is godly or biblical. During this time, God wanted to point out that 'without form...void' means chaos. Darkness is a biblical symbol of evil or wrong. Let there be light refers to God bringing light into darkness. Yes, God produced physical light. This light God commanded an established reality of humankind and animals. Therefore, *Tormented Dreams* demonstrates how dreams and/or visions become a reality (Daniel 9-12). The word light also refers to truth. Therefore, if we know the truth and study God's Word, we'll be able to overcome Satan's traps and bring things to light in this dark, evil world.

Roya Whitmore is the main character who has personal issues with believing her handsome husband will cheat on her even envisioning it in her dreams and visions. She struggles to accept her gift of visions and dreams whether it is from God or the Devil. Personal note: I blend and mesh with this character so well as if she was me, or dream to be, and connected to this character more than any I've ever written at this point.

Solomon Whitmore proves he is the head of the household and loves his wife dearly, more than life himself. He abides by the vows to cherish and love her like Jesus loves the church, and values her like his own body (Ephesians 5:25-33). He controls his temper at times when his wife takes him to the outer limits but still holds his own as her husband, friend, and lover.

Jewel, Roya's mother, is a fun character to write because she reminds me of my mother. However, of course, my mother has not done any of the things that Jewel has done in the book such as having an adulterous affair, wants all the pension monies, regardless of her adulterous past and gave birth to a child she hid from her immediate family including her militant husband. Ironically, she cannot handle what's dished out at her after she faces her consequences.

Other characters will shine in the next series. Roya Whitmore will always be there. Continue to dream.

Those titles are listed as follows:

Book 1: Tormented Dreams

Book 2: Outcry, Shalom!

Book 3: Marked Souls

Book 4: In the Nick of Time

Book 5: Diabolical Invasion

Book 6: Armageddon's Bloodshed

Book 7: Christ Coming

Author's Site: http://www.adriennaturner.net

In *Outcry, Shalom!*, the second book of Miss the Mark Series, Satan secretly comes to Earth shrouded in a diabolical force known as the Antichrist. Hailed as the Messiah by many, he sets up a task force before his arrival. Many will cry out for peace once some of the task force has unleashed their power.

How will Roya Whitmore and her family handle the challenges as the epic battle for dominion between Satan and God begins to heat up?

www.ingramcontent.com/pod-product-compliance
Lightning Source LLC
Chambersburg PA
CBHW020828260626
47169CB00003B/882